forgotten TALES of Colorado

Stephanie Waters

illustrations by

Kristen Solecki

THE History PRESS

Published by The History Press
Charleston, SC 29403
www.historypress.net

First published 2013

Manufactured in the United States

ISBN 978.1.60949.886.3

Library of Congress CIP data applied for.

Notice: The information in this book is true and complete to the best of our knowledge. It is offered without guarantee on the part of the author or The History Press. The author and The History Press disclaim all liability in connection with the use of this book.

To survivors and *The Misfits*

Contents

Acknowledgements

Thanks again to The History Press and especially to my commissioning editor, Becky Lejeune, who went to bat for me once again. I would also like to thank my editor, Will Collicott, and illustrator, Kristen Solecki, as well as the rest of the production team for making me look smart. Special thanks to the people I interviewed and to my globetrotting parents, who passed down their spirit of wanderlust. Special thanks also to family, friends, Siddhartha, Mary Jane and monkeys.

Introduction

They say that truth is stranger than fiction, and nowhere is that adage truer than in Colorado. If you don't believe me, then just tune into the crazy cartoon *South Park*, which regularly makes fun of Colorado's quirky history. The Centennial State has always been known for its wild stories, perhaps because of its culturally rich diversity. Several different Native American tribes called Colorado home, and both French and Spanish flags flew over the region long before American colors were officially hiked up the proverbial flagpole. Mining brought thousands of prospectors from all over the world, and storytelling around campfires became an integral part of Colorado's rich heritage.

I have always enjoyed fabled yarns about Colorado, and I especially love visiting the Centennial State's many ghost towns, quirky roadside attractions and oddball museums. My interest began as a youngster when I saw a stuffed two-headed calf exhibited at the Wonder Tower Museum in Genoa. Like my dad, I prefer black lining it on old forgotten highways whenever I take road trips. I laughed my head off the first time I heard of Oh My God Road; I thought the guy at the Idaho Springs gas station was just pulling my leg. It wasn't so funny when I actually traversed the high-altitude roller coaster ride from hell! Last August, I was black lining it with my Rottweiler and Maltipoo when, horror of all horrors, I broke down in the middle of nowhere. I didn't have cell phone service or a spare tire, but I figured I could always eat my dogs—if I really had to. It was getting dark when I happily spied lights off in the distance. My salvation was a little garage called, of all things, the Bloody Knuckle. Stranger still was the fact that the mechanic actually recognized me. Travis looked me up and down and then stared me straight in the eye and asked if I had ever been on America's Most Wanted. I thought he was joking, but he never batted an eye. Then the mechanic asked if my name was Stacy something, and I teased, "Only if you don't have a warrant!" The mechanic's wife, who introduced herself as "Wicked Wanda," also seemed to know me from somewhere. After a moment, she curiously asked if I was ever at Sturgis. I had to admit that I was—thirty years earlier, adding that I was a much younger man back in those days. The motorcycle mama ignored my joke and then hesitantly asked if I was a writer. Needless to say, I was so shocked that you could have pushed me over with a wet noodle. I was surprised to learn that the couple had gone on one of my haunted history tours and had read both my books. I basked in the glory of fame for a brief moment but tried not to let it show. I told the young couple that I was about to pen another book for The History Press to be called *Forgotten Tales of Colorado*. I excitedly explained that the book would be a compilation of amazing stories from long ago and would be kind of like a pulp tabloid for history geeks. To prove the stories were factual, I planned to include original newspaper headlines whenever possible. I added that this book, like my others, would also include a chapter about mad dogs and naked ladies, because everyone knows that sex and violence sell.

Travis went to tow my truck back to the Bloody Knuckle while Wanda showed me around their old homestead. When he returned, we joined him in the garage with beer and popcorn. We really enjoyed sitting around the warmth of the old pot-bellied stove while Travis patched my tire and told stories about his pioneer ancestors who homesteaded the property. The garage was piled high with rusted mechanical parts from everything from old cars to antique washing machines. The crafty mechanic had soldered some of the scraps together to create some rather interesting artwork. Especially enchanting was a life-size grizzly bear made from recycled bicycle parts. After a while, I noticed a mounted taxidermy head hanging high on the garage wall that looked like some kind of a weird, horned jackrabbit. Travis explained that the elusive creature was known as a jackalope and told of how his great-great-granddaddy shot the prized critter near the Platte River long ago. The couple then kindly invited me to go jackalope hunting with them the following weekend. I regretfully declined, saying that I had to get started writing my next book, but thanked them for their hospitality, warmly adding that you always meet the nicest folks in Colorado!

I hope you enjoy reading this collection of forgotten tales of Colorado as much as I did researching and writing them for your pleasure.

Chapter 1

Hunt and Pray

There is only one step from the sublime to the ridiculous.
—Napoleon Bonaparte

When the hunter becomes the hunted, there is a problem. Wild animals kill hunters every year in Colorado, yet the sport still grows in popularity. Elusive creatures are the most sought after and when mounted as trophy heads demand top dollar. Serious collectors of taxidermies are always looking to buy the mounted head of a horned rabbit known as the jackalope, or in Latin, *Lepus temperaentalus*. These cute bunnies seem harmless, but don't be fooled by the innocent look of this depraved fiend. The jackalope is well known for its needle-sharp teeth and painful, venomous bite. It makes you wonder why anybody would want to hunt such a dreadful creature, especially since there is not much meat on their scrawny bodies. But those lucky few who have actually tasted the tender flesh of the jackalope say that it is as succulent as prime veal and that sipping its milk is like drinking the nectar of the gods. Even today, outdoorsmen will tell you that they enjoy the challenge of hunting jackalopes over any other wild beast in Colorado. The little varmints are well known for their uncanny ability to mimic human voices and elude their predators by hiding in shrubbery and yelping phrases such as "I saw him go that-a-way!" and "Run, rabbit, run!" Cowboys on the trail used to tell of how jackalopes liked to hide in bushes around the campfire and sing backup while they strummed the guitar—a trick that the common, ignorant prairie dog could never master. Most of the time, the cowpokes didn't mind harmonizing with the horned bunnies, just as long as they kept a safe distance. After breaking camp, some of the cowboys would leave behind scrambled eggs, pancakes and a sip of whiskey as an offering to the mercurial varmints for not killing them in their sleep.

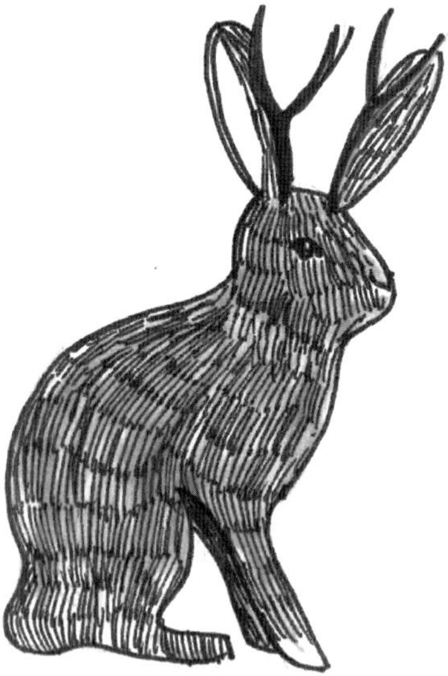

While every year thousands of hunters roam Colorado in search of elusive wild game, few of them have ever caught the sneaky Rocky Mountain snipe. The best time to hunt one of these tricky critters is at night during mating season.

Rocky Mountain snipes only mate during violent electrical storms—perhaps this hazardous habit explains why they are so few in number. No doubt these nocturnal critters are extremely difficult to capture, being that they are quick to the eye and slippery to the touch. So it was a huge surprise when a Greek agricultural student in Fort Collins captured three on one November night in 1912. The startling news made front-page headlines in the *Denver Post*, which shouted, "SNIPE HUNTER HOLDS BAG SO WELL THAT HE CATCHES THREE!"

Alonzo Paglitto was just off the train when fellow students harangued him into trying out the popular American sport of snipe hunting. Considered to be a right of passage, snipe hunting was sometimes used to initiate greenhorns into fraternities and other secret societies. Needless to say, being invited to a snipe hunt was a tried-and-true honor. Snipes belong to the weasel family and are said to resemble large ferrets. Snipes stink to high heaven but are easily skinned and make for good eating. With just a little patience, Rocky Mountain snipes are relatively easy to catch, but hunts can go on all night, and most folks give up long before sunrise. A hunting license is not required to catch a snipe, but you will need a gunnies sack, baseball bat and lots of patience. Initiates are instructed to hold the bag open while the more seasoned hunters round up the snipes by beating bushes and shooing them in the appropriate direction. After a snipe is bagged, the initiate whistles for the others, and then everyone goes to his house for breakfast to enjoy the fresh game. Sadly, snipe hunting is not always fun and games. An article in the *Aspen Daily Times* reported about a horrible incident with headlines that shouted:

JOKE ENDS IN TRAGEDY
SEVERAL MEN PARTICIPATE IN PRACTICAL JOKE
VICTIM SOUGHT REVENGE AND WAS FATALLY SHOT

Canadians Robert Morgan and his brother had recently moved to Telluride and were pleased as punch when asked by fellow sawmill employees to join them that evening for a Rocky Mountain snipe hunt. After holding the bag for six hours in the freezing cold, the Morgan brothers realized that they had been duped. When the angry brothers went to the foreman with their complaints about the bullies, his gut-wrenching laughter only added salt to their wounds. The next morning, the Morgan brothers went to their co-workers' bunkhouse demanding an apology, but the men just chuckled about the tomfoolery. Robert Morgan had had enough of the mockery and pulled a gun. Sadly, the Canadian was not fast enough, for the foreman fatally shot him before he even had the chance to say, "I hate Rocky Mountain snipe hunting!"

Chapter 2

Hook, Line and Sinker

I never lost a little fish—yes, I am free to say;
It always was the biggest fish I caught that got away.
—Eugene Field, "Our Biggest Fish"

Anglers are well known for telling whoppers, especially in Colorado, where seasoned fishermen never let the truth get in the way of a good fish story. One funny tale holds that during the winter of 1877–78, prospectors in the mining camp of Leadville ate so much venison that tallow stuck to their tongues and even piping hot coffee or hard liquor couldn't wash it away. The desperate men set candles on their heads, which melted the fat but caught their hair on fire, leaving them as bald as babies. Thankfully, a southern solicitor calling himself the "Miracle Man" came to town proudly sporting a bountiful crown of curls. The oldster accredited his youthful appearance to a powerful hair-growing tonic that he had invented. Three weeks later, the miners were as happy as pigs in mud when hair sprouted on their shiny noggins. One fateful morning, the miracle man was making a delivery and accidently fell into the river. Several jugs of the wonder tonic broke, and before you know it, fishermen started catching fur-bearing trout! Savvy anglers caught barrels of furry fish by using barber poles instead of standard fishing rods. Fishermen propped fake barber poles in the river and sang of free haircuts. Needless to say, the insidious scheme worked, but when mining tailings began clouding the water, the furry fish could no longer see the barber poles, and most of them eventually died off. Every once in awhile, you can still hear fishermen brag about catching furry trout—but they always seemed to get away.

Fishing was never easier than it was in Cripple Creek on August 25, 1911, when thousands of tiny fish fell from the heavens and splattered over the Union Baseball Field. Luckily, the fish storm happened during the seventh-inning stretch, and young whippersnappers were more than delighted to scoop up the guppy-sized grounders. According to the *Colorado Springs Gazette*, a carpenter living across from the ballpark collected over four bushels of fish from his yard and took them to Mayor F.A. Hassenplug, who just so happened to be an authority on such matters. After examining the mysterious bounty, the mayor determined that the fish were from the Atesco family—a saltwater species from the Pacific Ocean—and surmised that they were amazingly drawn up and carried into the clouds for thousands of miles before making a crash landing on the baseball field. Folks in downtown Colorado Springs were hardly impressed with Cripple Creek's crazy fishing story, probably because they were used to catching whoppers at home. A veritable angler's paradise was created in the Old North End neighborhood when water from Fountain Creek was pumped into irrigation canals that ran parallel with residential sidewalks. After a sizeable rainfall, these canals would often overflow onto lawns. Such was the case on Wednesday, July 2, 1919, when the *Gazette* headlined, "THREE-POUND FISH ON MINISTER'S LAWN PROVES SEASONS BEST FISH STORY."

Doctor Garvin, who resided on Cascade Avenue, remarked how surprised he was when a nineteen-inch rainbow trout volunteered to make him breakfast by literally swimming up to his kitchen door. He quipped that he had been fishing several times that summer but that it was the first time he caught anything big enough to sink his teeth into. The doctor knew no one would believe his good fortune, so he showed his prize to the next-door neighbor before frying it up in cornmeal and butter. According to the article, finding fish in the irrigation canals was quite common during the turn of the century, and in 1905, the slippery critters were so plentiful that they actually clogged the Evergreen Cemetery water hydrants!

The most surprising fish story has to do with prospector Joseph C. Jones, who moved into the territory in 1859 when he was just a pup. Like many others seeking riches during the Pikes Peak or Bust gold rush, Jones settled in Colorado

City, where he could prospect nearby. At the age of forty-three, the lifelong bachelor had saved $200 to purchase prime mountain property. On August 1, 1873, Jones christened the new township Jones Park, which included most of the eastern and southern slopes of Pikes Peak. Mr. Jones hoped to attract mountain-climbing enthusiasts, so he built a small lodge near the trail to Pikes Peak. As the years wore on, rumors swirled that the aging prospector had gone mad, and folks refused to go near his lodge. One of these people was the Reverend R.T. Cross, who wrote about a memorable encounter that he had with the owner of Jones Park in his autobiography, *My Mountains*, which was published in 1921. The reverend recalled that he had first encountered the crazy hermit during a crystal-hunting trip back in 1882. Despite his lunacy, Mr. Jones was quite hospitable and took great pride in showing off his rustic lodge, productive vegetable garden and a unique fishing pond that he made by diverting water from Bear Creek. Inside the pond were dozens of native greenback cutthroat trout that he had pilfered from the South Platte River. Sadly, the crazy old hermit died a month later, unaware of the amazing contribution that he inadvertently made to Colorado. According to a 2012 *Gazette* article, scientists were dumbfounded when a small pool of seventy native greenback cutthroat trout was found in a four-mile stretch of Bear Creek. That particular strain of the species had been declared extinct in 1937. Researchers compared DNA from gill clippings of the Bear Creek trout with historic

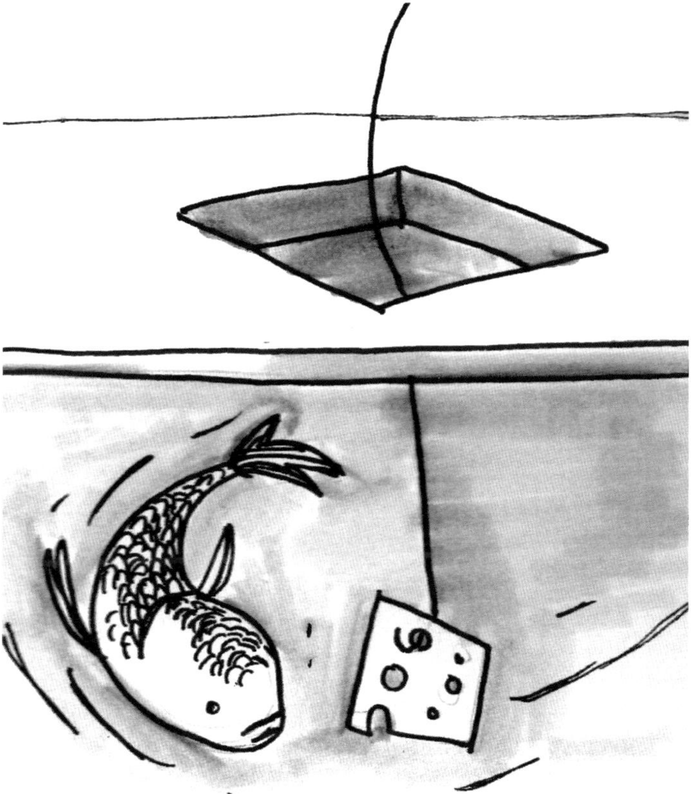

samples and agreed that the crazy old fisherman of Jones Park helped save the species from extinction. And that, my friend, is no fish tale!

In 1889, the National Fish Hatchery was established in Leadville, Colorado. It is the second-oldest operating hatchery in the United

States. Each year, the hatchery, along with the Colorado Division of Wildlife, stocks over 160,000 catchable trout into Colorado reservoirs. The historic hatchery also offers interesting tours. For more information, please call 719-486-0176.

Chapter 3

Holy Wonders

God performs in a mysterious way His wonders to perform.
—William Cowper

The name Colorado was chosen in 1861 by territory congressmen and is said to be Spanish in origin, meaning "colored red." The Centennial State has always been described as colorful, home to bright-red rock monoliths, majestic purple mountains, azure skies and electric orange sunsets. Katherine Lee Bates was so enraptured by the view from Pikes Peak that she later penned the spine-tingling anthem "America the Beautiful." The natural beauty of Colorado is truly awe inspiring—from its snow-capped mountains to the wind-swept prairies. The American Indians believed that Mother Nature was sacred, and especially beguiling were the plentiful mineral springs that miraculously bubbled from lakes, rivers and streams. One legend tells of an Indian chief on his deathbed who was ready to hang up his tomahawk but was miraculously healed after soaking in the mineral waters of Hot Sulphur Springs. Chief Ouray also enjoyed a good, hot bath now and then, and perhaps that is why his favorite mineral pools became known as Ouray Hot Springs. When the American Indians entered the valley named in honor of Algonquian Indian chief Manitou, it was considered sanctuary. Warring tribes knew to put down their weapons and wipe off their war paint, as the springs were a sacred gift from the gods. Early French trappers found baskets near the mineral springs that the Ute, Kiowa, Arapaho and Cheyenne left behind as holy offerings. In later years, the mineral water was blessed by priests and used in religious ceremonies all around the world. A May 3, 1922 article in the *Colorado Springs Gazette* headlined "MANITOU WATER FOR CHRISTENING."

Water was a big concern to Mother Cabrini, who unknowingly purchased barren property on the east slope of Lookout Mountain in 1902. Not finding even a drop of dew was somewhat of a problem, as the land had been purchased for a girls' camp. The legend holds that after Mother Cabrini realized her dilemma, she prayed for guidance. One morning, she awoke bright-eyed and bushy-tailed and climbed the mountain at sunrise. Upon reaching a shady grove, Mother Cabrini tapped her cane on a rock and confidently instructed the sisters to dig. Miraculously, as soon as the nuns rolled the stone over, water sprang forth from the ground to reveal a wondrous fountain of bubbling water. The sacred spring was housed in an eight-thousand-gallon tank generously donated by the nearby brewery of Adolph Coors. The miracle spring water has never stopped flowing—even through some rainless summers and winters with little snowfall. Many faithful pilgrims believe that the water is blessed with healing powers. They later built a shrine resembling the grotto of Lourdes, France, over the sacred spring as a place to go to seek peace and guidance. In 1954, a stunning twenty-two-foot statue called the "Sacred Heart of Jesus" was carved by an Italian artist and erected on the mountain. The proud monument towers over the canyon and can be seen for several miles. According to Jan Murphy's intriguing book *Mysteries and Legends of Colorado: True Stories of the Unsolved and Unexplained*, Mother Cabrini once wrote a letter to her former home in Italy that read in part:

> *The name Colorado was never better implied than to this enchanting country…to these most beautiful natural parks, where the hand of man could never add greater beauty than which nature has enriched it. In truth, here one exclaims spontaneously: How wonderful is God in his works!*

In 1912, after she was recognized by the pope as having performed a true miracle, Mother Francis Xavier Cabrini was the first American citizen to become a Catholic saint.

In 1963, another strange miracle occurred when long-dead roses, grown in the backyard of a Colorado Springs neighborhood, suddenly sprang back to life. The six long-stemmed American Beauties were grown by Mrs. Rose Arveson and were placed on her coffin during her funeral. After the services, Rose's adult children each took a keepsake rose and thought nothing more of it. Mysteriously, ten days

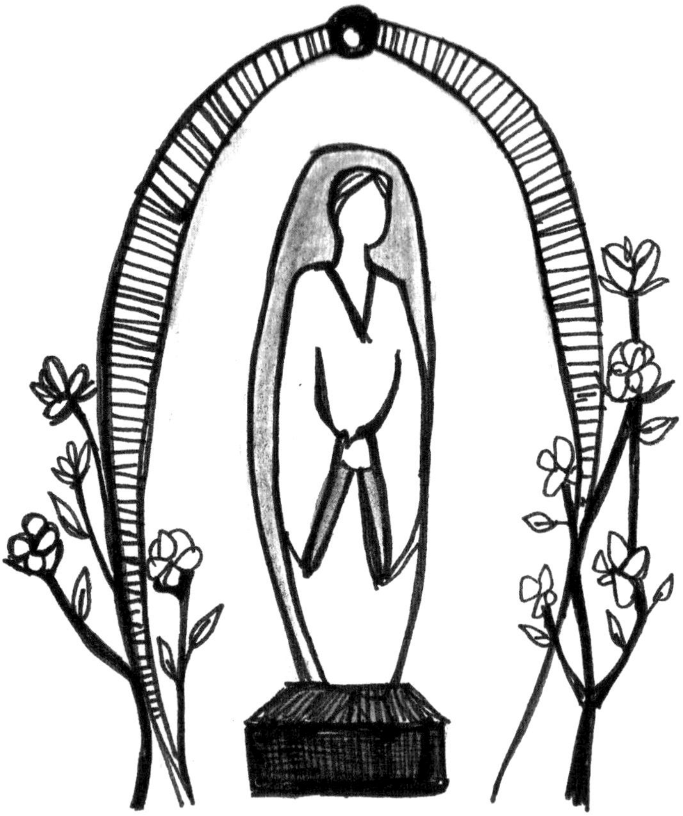

later, all six roses sprang back to life, more radiant than ever before, and the family was convinced it was a true miracle from God. The Arveson children were so impressed that they built a backyard shrine for their mother and opened it to the public. The Arveson Shrine of the Miracle Rose also featured life-size statues of Mother Mary, Jesus and several pious saints.

Word quickly spread near and far, and the shrine became infamous in tabloid newspapers such as the *National Enquirer*. The miracle shrine was even the topic of conversation around the dinner table at the White House. In fact, President Reagan wrote the Arveson children an impressive letter commending their efforts. In October 1986, the *Colorado Springs Gazette* headlined, "SPRINGS WOMEN BELIEVE THEIR MOM A SAINT."

Folks from all over the country made pilgrimages to the Arveson Shrine, hoping to be healed by holy roses grown from the miracle garden. Hundreds of people claimed to have been healed by the Arveson roses. Those who could not make the journey were sent rose petals in exchange for a small donation. Half a century later, the backyard shrine is still open to the public, although the roses are now strangled by weeds, and the saints don't stand as erect as they once did. The children of Rose Arveson were hoping to have their mother beatified, but their dreams never came to fruition. Perhaps it was a good thing that she was never granted the holy title. After all, there is no doubt that all moms are saints—but would you really want one who has actually been canonized?

The Ave Maria Shrine is a small stucco chapel that is perched on the side of a mountain overlooking the quaint village of Trinidad, Colorado. The legend of the holy monument holds that in 1908, Dr. John Epsy left the San Rafael Hospital during a snowstorm hoping to make it home before dinner. Tragically, the blizzard worsened, causing his horse-and-buggy to careen into a ditch. As the snow deepened and the sky darkened, the good doctor knew that he needed to find shelter. Epsy wandered for hours but was unknowingly moving in circles. The doctor feared that death was imminent, yet he continued to mumble prayers, fervently hoping for a miracle. Just then, he saw a mysterious light off in the distance. Doctor Epsy took a leap of faith and struggled toward the radiant beam, which led him to a protective alcove. Miraculously, inside the niche was a glowing candle flickering beneath a statue of Mother Mary. Doctor Epsy hovered close to the holy relic throughout the bitter cold night and was grateful to be rescued early the next morning. Years later, the Ave Maria Shrine was built to house the statue of the blessed mother on the very spot where Epsy found it.

Lo and behold, yet another miracle happened in Trinidad during the summer of 1866, when George Simpson and his young daughter were being chased by the Indians but managed to elude the savages by ducking into a cave overlooking the village. When their lives were spared, Simpson declared it to be a profound miracle and later told his wife that when the time came, he wanted to be buried on the mountain that saved his life. Twenty years later, George's wish was granted, and when his daughter died two years after him, she, too, was buried on a spot now called Simpson's Rest. I guess you could say that many miracles have occurred in the southern hub of Trinidad, especially at the formerly mentioned Mount San Raphael Hospital. The historic hospital is famous for more than its location next to the holy Ave Maria Shrine. Believe it or not, Mount San Raphael has performed more sex-change operations than any other hospital on the planet. It's uncanny to think that the ancient village of Trinidad, with its charming ivy-laced cottages, white picket fences and worn brick lanes, is now known as the so-called sex change capital of the world. But like they say, God works in mysterious ways.

The Trinidad History Museum is a must-see. For more information, please call 719-846-7217.

Chapter 4

Mad Medicine

There are some remedies worse than disease.
—Publilius Syrus

Several early physicians in Colorado made medical history. Dr. Rice of Twin Lakes was known for making house calls from his traveling cabin. The doctor built his office on a sled, which was complete with a pot-bellied stove with a rusty smoke pipe that twisted out of the roof. The good doctor steered his ski-house through an opening in which his horses were reined. In Telluride, Dr. George C. Balderson saved his own life by removing his appendix after realizing that he was the only man in town qualified to do the job. Doc Bailey of Montgomery was known for preserving a man's head in a glass jar that was proudly displayed in his office window. Folks around town joked that the pickled noggin belonged to a former deadbeat patient, but most thought the gruesome exhibit was just poor advertising. Decorated war hero Dr. Isaac Davis became better known as Dr. Frankenstein after creating an authentic human mummy. Davis was the distinguished coroner of El Paso County, so finding corpses to experiment on was a piece of cake. Unlucky Tom O' Neil, Dr. Davis's first victim, was stripped, shaved, soaked in a secret sauce for three hours a day and then strapped to a drying board. The naked dead man was then propped in front of the doctor's drugstore and allowed to dry in the afternoon sun—much to the horror of the townsfolk. Yet no one in Manitou could complain, as Dr. Davis was also the town's mayor and chief of police! Needless to say, finding a good doctor wasn't always easy in the early West—in fact, many physicians were un-licensed frauds. These unscrupulous con artists often dispensed homemade elixirs that were sometimes more hazardous than whatever ailed the patient. Such was the case reported in the May 11, 1911 issue of the *Denver Post*, which ran a story with the headline, "INDIAN MEDICINE KILLS RANCHER."

A twenty-three-year-old Woodland Park rancher known as Slim Jim complained that he was famished all the time. Jim ate like a bear but was as skinny as a string bean. A doctor diagnosed the long-legged cowboy as having a tapeworm living in his gut and quipped that it must have been at least three feet long, considering Jim's towering height. Hoping to cure the malady, the rancher's mother ordered a powerful potion from a witch doctor. The strange

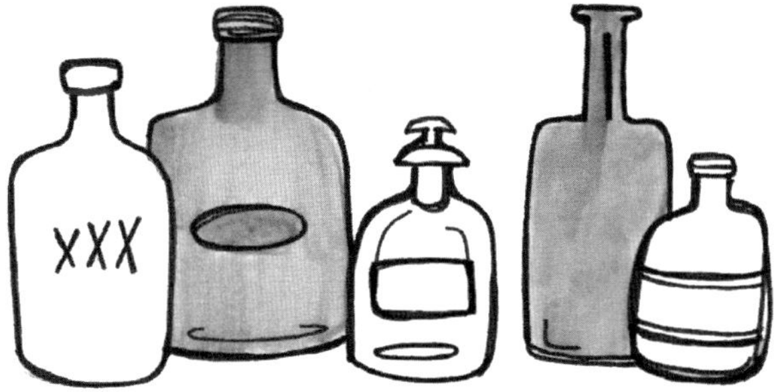

brew eliminated the monstrous tapeworm as promised… but tragically killed Slim Jim along with it.

However, not all doctors were uneducated and corrupt. One well-respected pioneer physician was Dr. Susan Anderson, who hung her shingle in Cripple Creek for a spell. Doc Suzie was made famous in the television series *Dr. Quinn Medicine Woman*, which was loosely based on her life story. Cripple Creek was also the first town in Colorado in which a licensed medical doctor sanctioned the use of Madstone Magic to cure the deadly mad dog disease. The story begins in 1898 when neighbors in Colorado City were worried about Jesse James and his dirty deeds. Jesse James was a mutt whose owners kept with the tradition of naming a good dog after a bad man. Jesse, however, was not anywhere close to being good—in fact, he was just bad to the bone. The vile creature frothed at the mouth, jumped tall fences, demolished flowerbeds, killed cats and stunk to high heaven! The dog's weary owners tried everything they could think of to keep the hapless hound from wandering. They even went to the drastic measure of putting gunpowder in his food—but that only gave the mutt terrible gas. Eventually, the dog's tail was cut off and nailed to the back gate, but even that old hillbilly trick failed to domesticate the calamitous canine. Mrs. Glenn Cameron was particularly leery of Jesse James, as the dog often lurked behind her back fence. One fateful afternoon, the savage beast bit the schoolteacher when she tried to stop him from fornicating with her poodle. Mrs. Cameron scrubbed the wound clean but still worried about the injury. As a safety precaution, the young woman procured a snippet of hair from the dog that bit her and gulped it down with a teaspoon of turpentine, hoping beyond reason that the ancient folk remedy would work its magic.

The next morning, when the teacher awoke with a milky white tongue and a high fever, she feared the worst. Mrs. Cameron knew the early symptoms of mad dog disease and was convinced that she needed a madstone to save her life. Madstones were found in the bellies of grazing animals, and the most powerful came from an albino deer, also known as a "witch deer." These mysterious speckled rocks were basically just balls of calcified hair, grass and dirt. Some of these mystical stones were found when gutting an animal, but most were passed down from father to son or inherited from other family members. Needless to say, genuine madstones were prized family heirlooms that were well guarded and highly sought after. Despite being well educated, Mrs. Cameron believed in the power of madstones and was elated to learn of an old man living nearby who owned one. The schoolteacher boiled the palm-sized rock in a pot of sweet milk just as the old man instructed, but the milk didn't turn green like it was supposed to, and the madstone wouldn't latch onto the dog bite. When Mrs. Cameron returned the rock, she learned why it failed to work its magic. Apparently, the old man had paid big bucks for the treasure, unaware that madstones lost their magic if ever bought or sold.

Thankfully, the desperate schoolteacher heard about a medicine woman in Cripple Creek who owned a mighty powerful madstone. Mrs. W.S. Driver met Mrs. Cameron at the train station and then rushed her to Dr. Denny, who was already boiling the madstone. Once the milk turned green, the hot rock was placed onto the gaping wound. Within seconds, the porous stone latched onto the infected dog bite and suckled it like a newborn babe. Believe it or not, that darn madstone remained suctioned to Mrs. Cameron's hand for three days and would not come off even while sleeping, eating, washing dishes or bathing! On the fourth day, the mysterious rock suddenly rolled to the floor as if it were gorged and exhausted. Dr. Denny was called to do a physical examination and proclaimed that Mrs. Cameron was as fit as a fiddle. Word of the strange poison-sucking rock spread near and far, and the townsfolk were both relieved and amazed that the crazy treatment actually worked. On November 2, 1898, the *Colorado Springs Gazette Telegraph* performed an investigation on the strange incident and reported its results in an article headlined, "AUTHENTICATED CASE OF A CURE WITH A MADSTONE."

Mrs. Driver claimed that she had inherited six magic stones with various healing powers and noted that it was the first time she knew of a madstone being used in Colorado. A few years back, she used a madstone in Arkansas when a wild dog bit an old man and his cow. She treated the oldster with a madstone, and he lived, but the poor heifer died the very next day. The experience convinced her of the stones' magical powers, and it was all the proof the medicine woman needed. The newspaper concluded the jaw-dropping story by quoting Dr. Denny as saying, "I believe in them [madstones]. This my first experience with that black object, stone or whatever it may be. I wanted to test those so-called madstones, and I can tell you now that I am satisfied."

So just remember that if you ever happen to be snooping around granny's attic and stumble across a box of speckled black rocks, you may have just found the family jewels.

For more information on haunted history walking tours of Old Colorado City, please contact Colorado Ghost Tours at 719-685-2409.

Chapter 5

The Ape Man and Bigfoot

Man is equally incapable of seeing the nothingness from which he emerges and the infinity in which he is engulfed.
—Blaise Pascal

Most people will agree that there is more in the world that we don't understand than what we do. This was certainly true in Fairplay, Colorado, where legends of a wild Ape Man creature haunted folks for many years. Rumors were that the mysterious half-man/half-beast hunted wild game in the dense forest at night. Several witnesses had seen the elusive creature and believed it to be an old woman's exotic pet. Sheriff Richards didn't accept any of the hogwash, but when tensions mounted, he felt obligated to perform a standard investigation. In the summer of 1928, the sheriff went about the county interviewing folks about the strange creature until he finally ended up at widow Beeler's expansive ranch. The reclusive Mrs. Beeler was sitting on her front porch when the sheriff arrived but didn't speak much or offer assistance in his search. When the lawman went around to the back of the house, he was puzzled to smell a foul odor and hear noises coming from a stone shed. The lawman suspected that a skunk might be stuck inside and braced himself before looking in the window. However, nothing could have prepared him for what he was about to see next—staring right back at him was a wild-eyed man-beast shackled to the wall. The hairy creature growled fiercely and rattled the chains, which caused the frightened lawman to nearly wet his britches! Mrs. Beeler Walked up and tearfully explained that the wild man was actually her forty-five-year-old son, adding that imprisonment was the only way that she knew to control him. The old woman cooed that he was a beautiful baby but had turned like soured milk once he reached puberty. She then grimly added that her boy hadn't worn any clothes or had a bath in over a decade. The sheriff almost laughed when Mrs. Beecher told him that the wild man's name was Harry, and newspapers all across the country had a field day with the strange story. On August 22, 1928, the *Denver Post* stunned its readers with the freaky headline, "MOTHER FEARS APEMAN."

The sheriff's investigation was a Godsend, and "Harry the Ape Man" was sent to the Pueblo State hospital, where he got a much-needed shave and shower. Mrs. Beeler was never charged for imprisoning her wild teenager, and she received an outpour of sympathy from understanding mothers all across the country. Even though this particular account of the

Ape Man was explained, many others never were. In October 1922, the *Salt Lake Telegram* headlined an interesting article with a caption that frightened folks in Utah: "WEIRD TALES OF WILD CREATURE SEEN IN COLORADO."

A wild monster was ravaging animals on the western slope of Colorado in the Naturita Valley. According to an eyewitness, the hairy creature had large, fiery eyes that flashed from beneath a heavy brow. The strange beast hunted wild game at night, and the gruesome evidence of half-eaten carcasses often littered the mountainsides in the mornings. When game was scarce, the wild man began devouring domestic animals, much to the horror of local ranchers. The beast raided smokehouses, gardens, cellars, chicken coops and barns and devoured everything, including guard dogs! It appeared that no living thing was safe from the creature's volcanic appetite, and everyone began to fear the mysterious tyrant. Finally, a few ranchers declared war. Plans were made to capture and sell the wild Ape Man to the circus. The *Aspen Daily Times* reported in July 1904 with a blaring headline that warned:

WILD MAN IN TAYLOR PARK
WHEN HE STANDS UPRIGHT, HE IS
SEVEN FEET TALL WITH A LONG,
HAIRY MANE

According to the article, several well-known ranchers cornered the wild beast and tried to lasso him into a cage,

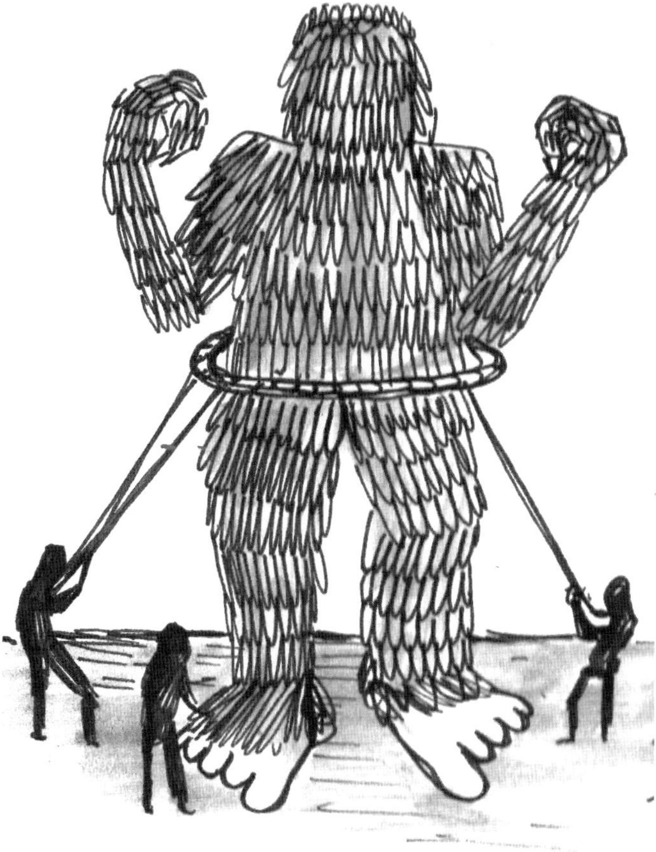

but the creature managed to elude them and escaped into the hills without a trace.

The northern American Indians passed down legends about an immense half-man/half-beast with long, shaggy arms, calling him Sasquatch. Other American Indian tribes across the United States also told similar tales about the mythical Ape Man, and in the South, he was known as the Skunk Ape. Some legends told that this wild monster survived on human flesh, while others told that the creature was not an animal at all but actually a benevolent being from another spiritual realm. According to local legend, even the famous scout Kit Carson reported seeing the elusive creature in Park County but didn't know what to call it. It was not until the 1950s that the term Bigfoot was officially coined to describe the mysterious creature. Identifying and then agreeing on a name was the first step in trying to understand the misunderstood monster. Those who seriously study the Bigfoot phenomena call themselves cryptozoologists, and some argue that perhaps the Ape Man and Bigfoot are one and the same species.

The Bigfoot legend is so popular in Colorado that when you drive up Pikes Peak, you just might notice a sign warning that the area is home to the legendary monster. The average tourist might just scoff at the Bigfoot crossing signs, not realizing that they are not a joke. On December 7, 1992, the *Colorado Springs Gazette* featured an article about Bigfoot sightings in the Pikes Peak region. The article was headlined, "BIGFOOT JUST ONE OF LIFE'S MYSTERIES." According to the article, there were quite a few folks in the Pikes Peak region who had encounters with Bigfoot, and one Green Mountain Falls resident, Dan Masias, had even acquired actual proof of its existence.

One night in July 1988, Masias was awakened by a loud noise and saw two apelike creatures running by his cabin window. The next morning, he photographed several extra large human-like footprints that were left behind in the snow. Curiously, one of the creatures actually snagged his hairy heiny, leaving a hunk of black fur stuck in a screen door. Professional lab results concluded that the hairball was of an unknown primate and could not be identified with any creature on the planet. Over the years, the retired researcher has spent thousands of dollars rigging special infrared cameras to various trees around his property and claims to have captured several photographs of Bigfoot, as well as hundreds of other unexplainable pictures. For the past twenty-five years, Masias has worked tirelessly to shed light on the ancient mystery, and he firmly believes that his property is located on some sort of a paranormal portal through which Bigfoot travels into other dimensions. Masias has been featured on CNN, *Unsolved Mysteries*, Animal Planet and national radio programs as well.

Cripple Creek Museum docent Leon Drew is another resident of the Pikes Peak region who is a confirmed believer in Bigfoot. In January 2010, Mr. Drew spotted what he called a juvenile Bigfoot crossing Highway 67 near Gillette Flats and then again in the same place the following year. Just last spring, the nature buff was hiking in the Pikes Peak National Forest when he briefly came face to face with what he described as a large female Bigfoot, and now he never goes hiking without a camera! Leon didn't believe in Bigfoot before but now thinks the mysterious creature could possibly be the missing link of human evolution. Mr. Drew is so convinced of his theory that he has begun sponsoring annual Bigfoot conventions in Cripple Creek, where like-minded folks from all over the country gather to share evidence and discuss the science of cryptozoology. No matter what you believe about the mysterious Ape Man, one thing is for certain—the legend of Bigfoot is still alive and well in Colorado.

For more information on Bigfoot, please contact Pikes Peak Cryptozoological Research at 719-422-3668.

Chapter 6

Tesla and Extraterrestrials

To confine our attention to terrestrial matters would be to limit human spirit.
—Stephen Hawking

Colorado is home to the most phenomenal but extremely dangerous lightning storms, some of which come out of the clear blue sky. On a beautiful sunny day in June 1934, a young shepherd was mysteriously found dead near Burlington. Coroners were puzzled until they took into account the sixty dead sheep lying next to the man and figured lightning was to blame. In 1910, as the marching band played and banners waved over Eastonville, seven people were zapped dead by a surprise bolt just as King Spud was being crowned at the popular potato festival. That same summer, a fourteen-year-old girl made embarrassing headlines in Colorado Springs when the *Gazette* featured an article that August that bluntly stated the naked truth: "LIGHTNING DISROBES GIRL."

Mabel and her younger sister were staying at their grandparents' house when a lighting bolt suddenly ripped down the chimney and struck the girl, zapping her clothes from her body and leaving her completely nude. Other than being shocked by the surreal experience, the girl said that she felt fine but was very relieved that her boyfriend wasn't visiting at the time. Apparently being disrobed by lightning was not unusual in Colorado Springs, because on August 30, 1903, the *Gazette* featured another rather humiliating story with headlines that read, "STRIPPED OF HIS CLOTHING BY LIGHTNINGS FLASH."

Pikes Peak Cog Railway engineer Art Bruer told reporters that the cog train was loaded with passengers and was about to leave the summit when a vicious lightning bolt came out of the clear blue sky, striking him from the train and the clothes from his body. Someone noticed that the young man's fleece underwear was afire and doused him with water to put out the flames. Naturally, spectators believed the smoldering man was dead until he sat up and asked for more water. A concerned gift shop employee gave the engineer a cup of hot chocolate and propped the scorched engineer's cap back on his head. Art was redder than the Navajo blanket wrapped around him but took the embarrassing situation in stride. As the engineer drove the tourists back down the mountain, he made jokes about his ridiculous impromptu uniform. Reporters, who had already lined up and were awaiting his arrival, asked what it felt like to be struck by lightning. Art recounted how he had seen a flash of light, heard a thunderous clap and felt like someone slapped him on the face. At least the engineer's employers rewarded him for his shocking bravery and for taking it on the chin.

Electrical engineer Nikolas Tesla was greatly inspired by the effects of lightening, and so he moved to Colorado in the late 1800s to study the thrilling natural phenomena. The handsome Croatian became well known for being somewhat of an arrogant mad scientist. The lifelong bachelor moved to the mountain town of Ames, located near Telluride. During this time, Tesla attended a conference along with the up-and-coming Thomas Edison during which he championed the use of alternating current. Edison believed that working with alternating current (AC) was dangerous, calling it the "death beam." Obviously, Tesla's theory won out over Edison's, but the cocky Croatian never got the accolades he knowingly deserved for creating wireless signals. However, Tesla did get the attention of mega millionaire J.P. Morgan, who financed a laboratory in Colorado Springs. Tesla hoped to communicate with aliens by sending radio waves into the universe from the eighty-foot tower. The "Pikes Peak to Paris" plan was launched when Tesla sent 130-foot-long man-made lighting bolts through the midnight sky, rattling nearby houses and causing quite a stir in the neighborhood. The wireless message didn't reach Parisians or extraterrestrials, but it did manage to blow out the Colorado Springs power plant. Tesla got the message loud and clear when he was forced to rebuild the generator before leaving the city. Perhaps communicating with both Parisians and Martians was a stretch, but Colorado was still an ideal location to perform the crazy experiments. The Centennial State has always been well known for its many cosmic sightings. Long ago, the American Indians told of the mystical "sky people" who sailed in airships. Several early newspapers recounted stories about mysterious aircraft even before man learned how to fly. On April 20, 1897, the *Rocky Mountain News* featured a story with the following headline:

MYSTERIOUS AIRSHIP
CRIPPLE CREEK CITIZENS VIEW A VERY STRANGE ROVER FLOATING OVER THE GOLD CAMP

For several weeks, residents of Nebraska, Kansas and Colorado witnessed a mysterious aircraft circling the skies. On August 19, a large crowd in Cripple Creek was treated to an up-close-and-personal experience with the same mysterious aircraft. When the noon service let out from church that Sunday, one parishioner noticed a strange bright light dancing over the gold camp. Within ten minutes, over five hundred people crowded around the corner of Third and Bennett Avenues to observe a strange cigar-shaped silver airship draw closer and then hover just a half mile above them. The aircraft revolved in slow intervals and radiated strange sounds. Churchgoers must have thought they were witnessing the second coming as they watched the mysterious light glide ominously above them. A few moments later, the vessel disappeared over Mineral Hill, much to the relief of the ever-growing crowd. After the spectacular show was over, many of the awestruck witnesses scrambled back into the church, fervently repeating their prayers. Just a few days later, headlines in the *Aspen Daily Times* reported:

MYSTERIOUS AIRSHIP
IT PASSED OVER ASPEN YESTERDAY MORNING

The first to notice the aircraft was a group of twenty miners that had just finished the night shift. Not a star could be seen as the snow fell that early morning, but a strange, bright light was observed hovering just above them. Several of the men noted how intense the light was and that it was bigger and brighter than a locomotive's headlamp. For the previous six weeks, hundreds of witnesses across the nation had seen the same silver cigar-shaped airship hovering in the skies. A farmer in Kansas reported that he accidently came upon the airship when it was resting in his wheat field but that he didn't notice it until it frightened his mule, which threw him in a ditch. The bewildered farmer watched in awe as the strange airship rose straight up from the ground and into the heavens within seconds. Government officials explained the mystery by stating that the vessel was just a kite used to measure meteorological conditions. However, the *Aspen Daily Times* stubbornly argued that the simple explanation was absurd and noted that several witnesses had field glasses and could see the craft in great detail. Hot-air balloons were ruled out as an explanation because they cannot stop or change direction, and they intermittently flashed fire from the hot air pump rather than a constant stream of light, as described by witnesses. On June 5, 1919, another article appeared in the *Pueblo Chieftain*, which reported that hundreds of witnesses in Colorado Springs, Pueblo, Florence and Canon City had seen another unexplained aircraft. The headlines blared, "STRANGE LIGHT MYSTIFIES PEOPLE IN FOUR CITIES."

Mike Colletta, also known as the UFO Geek, and his sidekick, Brett Leal, have been studying the night skies for over three decades. The space hounds have been featured on national radio and television programs to discuss their theories and reveal their purported evidence. Coletta and Leal are totally convinced that extraterrestrials have visited Colorado on many occasions. When asked if the strange lights seen over a century ago could have simply been the Aurora Borealis, both men confirmed that it would be very unlikely given the season and location of the sightings. The UFO experts note that Colorado is home to more UFO sightings than any other state in the country and that most are seen in the mysterious San Luis Valley. This high alpine

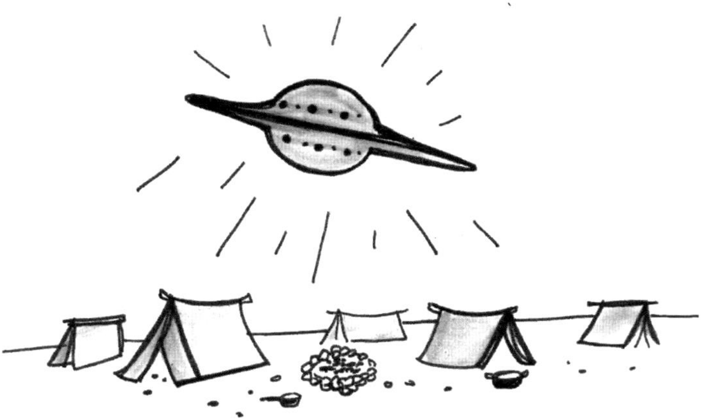

desert valley located in Southern Colorado has always been known for its mysteries, and one of the oldest dates back to 1853 with the legend of San Acacio. The legend holds that while men were working in the field, the Ute Indians took advantage of the situation and attacked the village. Just before the warring tribe was about to torch the town, the defenseless women and children prayed feverishly for a miracle—and got it! Amazingly, storm clouds suddenly parted, and an army of shimmering clad warriors swept through the heavens. The rebels, who were obviously frightened by the ominous apparition, made a hasty retreat. Today, many UFO aficionados believe that the ghostly sky warriors were actually extraterrestrials.

When dairy farmer Judy Messoline moved into the valley, she didn't believe in flying saucers or little green men until she witnessed a silver, cigar-shaped spacecraft fly within a stone's throw of her ranch house. Days later, she learned that one of her neighbor's cows had been carefully dissected with the precision of a surgeon. Local authorities found that the blood had been completely drained from the carcass, and radiation levels were measured around the animal. Judy learned that the area was infamous for its UFO sightings and cattle mutilations, which UFO aficionados believe are connected. A few years later, after her dairy ranch failed to be the cash cow she was hoping for, the enterprising rancher turned a portion of land into a UFO watchtower, campground and gift shop. Judy's neighbors must have thought she was losing it when she opened the far-out tourist attraction back in 2000, but she's been over the moon ever since. Judy claims to have had her photo taken with thousands of tourists from all over the world—and even with a few strangers who claimed to be visiting from other planets. If you think about it, extraterrestrials visiting Colorado sounds plausible since it's always been a vacation hotspot. Perhaps the little green men were just responding to the long-distance call Tesla sent to the Martians more than a century ago!

For more information on UFOs, check out UFOGEEK.com.

Chapter 7

Treasure Tales

Riches are gotten with pain, kept with care and lost with grief.
—Anonymous

Adventurous souls and those young at heart have always enjoyed dreaming about long-lost treasure. Colorado is well known for its legendary treasure tales, some of which go as far back as the sixteenth century. The legend of La Caverna del Oro, or Cave of Gold, tells that an Indian tribe passed guardianship of a sacred cave from one generation to the next for centuries. The Indians feared an evil curse put on the so-called Devil's Cave but knew that it held a golden treasure. Spanish monks convinced the Indians to lead them to the mysterious cavern, promising to remove the curse on the cave. After an arduous journey up the thirteen-thousand-foot Marble Mountain, the holy men were tickled pink to find a wooden door leading to riches beyond their wildest dreams. Once the cave was discovered, the Indian guides were forced to mine gold for the Spaniards. One day, the Indians staged a surprise revolt, killing everyone except for a monk by the name of De la Cruz. The lone monk used the victims' blood to mark a Maltese cross at the cave's exit and then loaded his horse with baskets of gold before fleeing back to Mexico. In 1869, Captain Elisha Horn inadvertently discovered the Devil's Cave when he found a skeleton clad in a rusty suit of armor lying near the mysterious Maltese cross. Apparently, the Spaniard had been murdered while guarding the treasure cave—an Indian arrow still protruded from the skeleton's bony neck. In the 1920s, a mountain ranger interviewed a 105-year-old Indian woman who said that the cave was always known to be haunted and that as a child, she remembered foolhardy miners leaving La Caverna del Oro with wagonloads of gold. The brave ranger, along with a few members from his mountain-climbing club, explored the cave and to their amazement found a 200-year-old rope ladder and a fifteenth-century hammer. Over the years, other courageous spelunkers have found shovels, clay jugs, arrowheads—and a human skeleton dangling by a chain clamped around its neck! Locals state that the bloodstained cross can still be seen near the exit of the cave, although no one has ever found the entrance or the mysterious door leading to the dazzling room of riches.

With all the outlaw activity going on in the early West, there were obviously several stories about stolen loot being stashed away in them thar hills. Perhaps the most fascinating story is about a rebel gang that was headed by the notorious Jim Reynolds. The cowboy moved to Fairplay hoping to strike it rich during the 1859 gold rush but turned to crime after becoming disillusioned by the slings and arrows of outrageous fortune. Jim was sent to the pokey but soon escaped and returned home to Texas toward the end of the Civil War. The renegade convinced twenty or so ruffians to join his crusade to raise money for the flailing Confederacy. The merry band of thieves, who were full of piss and vinegar, took the road to perdition—all the way to Colorado. The bandits delighted in robbing stage lines, wagon trains and other travelers along the way. Legend holds that the infamous bandits stashed a bank box filled with gold coins at their hideout on Kenosha Pass near Fairplay. One night, the camp was raided by law dogs, and Jim's right-hand man was killed and hastily buried under a tree. A buck knife was stuck into its trunk as a marker. Not long after, Jim Reynolds and a few gang members were sent up the river. However, the Union sympathizers who were supposed to be escorting the felons to prison secretly executed them along the way. A few years later, $80,000 in gold was found buried in an old fruit cellar on the Guiraud ranch, where the gang sometimes holed up, and many believed it was a small token of gratitude from the notorious Reynolds gang. Twenty years ago, a man was hiking near Handcart Gulch when he stumbled upon a primitive corral and found a rusty buck knife stuck in a tree trunk. The history buff guessed that it was the old outlaw

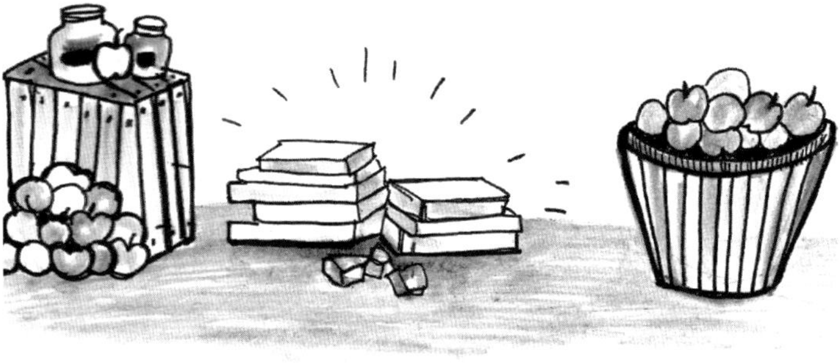

camp, and after the word got out, treasure hunters scoured the area, but the buried loot was never found.

One curious treasure tale involves a peculiar prospector named Alex Cobsky, who was orphaned as a child and preferred the company of animals to humans ever since. When he was still wet behind the ears, Cobsky began prospecting near the village of La Veta, where he made a few small claims over the years. All the women in town fought over the handsome and mysterious bachelor, but Cobsky never acted interested in women or friends of any kind. The solitary man eventually had a family of his own—two goats, a burrow and a couple of cute chicks—who all shared his humble straw bed. Cobsky's pampered pets enjoyed more than just the basic creature comforts, especially after they moved into the small cabin he built. Stories claim that the ruggedly handsome man never kissed a girl—likely because he lived in an animal house and only bathed but once a year. In 1901, the middle-aged miner was in hog heaven when his ore was evaluated at a Pueblo smelting plant as the richest ever found in Colorado. When the news made national headlines, Cobsky didn't take kindly to all the attention and high tailed it home before other gold diggers caught wind of his good fortune. Later that spring, the prosperous prospector returned to Pueblo with another bountiful load and earned even more cash than he did on the first trip. Rumors persisted that son-of-a-gun had rediscovered the lost Simpson Mine, whose owners were thought to have been killed by Indians years earlier. When news of the possible rediscovery spread, Cobsky became insanely protective of his riches and made even fewer trips into town. Stories were that the miserly miner booby-trapped his barn house, hoping to protect his hard-won fortune. For nearly forty years, the mysterious prospector never staked a claim. He protected the mine's whereabouts and willingly took his secret to the grave. Tragically, the seventy-nine-year-old Cobsky was riding his beloved Bessie when he was hit by a car. The mule survived, but the miner succumbed to his injuries one year later. On March 11, 1937, the *State Times Advocate* from Baton Rouge, Louisiana, published a story about the enigma with the headline, "TWO WOMEN LURED TO COLORADO BY PROSPECTOR'S STORY OF GOLD MINE.

The Pueblo hospital contacted the hermit's only known relatives—nieces Elizabeth Weibelt and Anna Reich—who were interviewed by the newspaper. The sisters said that they rarely saw their beloved uncle but remembered how the hermit would give them gold nuggets to cut their teeth on when they were youngsters. The sisters claimed that their uncle never divulged the source of his secret fortune to anyone and quoted him as saying, "It's been mine all of these years, and it will be mine when I'm buried." Even to this day, the mysterious mine, which was lost then found and lost once again, remains an elusive treasure trove of unclaimed riches.

Several other Colorado caves are known to be haunted, specifically the Cave of the Winds in Manitou Springs. Professional ghost hunters Christopher Allen Brewer and James Manda were featured on a program about the haunted cave on the Biography's My Ghost Story. *You can reach them at thespiritchasers@blogspot.com.*

The Francisco Fort Museum at 306 South Main Street in La Veta is loaded with interesting history. For more information, please call 719-640-5380.

Chapter 8

Cosmic Cobblers

All that we see or seem is but a dream within a dream.
—Edgar Allan Poe

The mid-1880s was a memorable time for tourism in the state of Colorado. A colossal nine-story ice palace was constructed in the mining town of Leadville. The attraction spread over five acres and included a restaurant, ballroom, indoor toboggan runs and an indoor ice-skating rink the size of two football fields! Inside, the shimmering ice walls featured all sorts of frozen oddities, including trophy-sized trout, American Beauty roses and bottles of Coors beer. The amazing winter castle was considered the largest ice sculpture ever created. The ambitious project began in early November and was constructed from five thousand tons of ice. The palace opened on New Year's Day in 1896 and attracted tourists from all over the world. The spectacular architectural feat is still remembered for its inspired yet fleeting beauty. The Leadville ice castle may have been the most popular tourist attraction in Colorado during that time, but it was not considered the most bizarre. Over sixty thousand people went to Denver to visit a shoe cobbler, and it wasn't just to have their heels resoled. Many claimed that the humble shoe repairman was a gifted healer, and Mr. Fox, a Denver city alderman, surely agreed. Fox claimed to have been cured from deafness after meeting the enigmatic cobbler in New Mexico, and so he invited the holy man to help others in the Mile High City. Francis Schlatter (sometimes spelled Schlader) carried a mysterious copper wand that he waved over the masses like a symphony conductor. The man of few words once explained to reporters that he used the wand as a healing tool. The holy healer also cured the sick with the power of touch. The cobbler possessed a gentle voice; long, dark hair; and large, expressive eyes. Not only did Francis Schlatter look like the common idea of Jesus; the humble cobbler also declared that he was actually the son of God—and thousands of people believed him! On August 10, 1895, the *Rocky Mountain News* featured one of many stories about the handsome stranger with headlines that read:

SCHLADER'S DELUSIONS
STRANGE HULLUCINATION OF DENVER COBBLER
THINKS HE IS THE CHRIST

HE TELLS AN ENQUIRER THAT HE DIED ON CALVARY

The holy healer never accepted gifts or payments, and thousands of people claimed to have been healed by the miraculous man. Crowds lined up around the block, but the average wait to see the healer was two to three days, so large tents were set up for lodging. The cosmic cobbler drew so much attention that he eventually caused problems for the city of Denver when both traffic and sewage backed up around the Fox home. In November, the Jesus wannabe suddenly left Denver, leaving behind only a note explaining that his heavenly father had called him home. Francis Schlatter was later seen in other big cities in which he also healed the masses and backed up sewage lines. For years, there were several imposters claiming to be the holy wonder, but it is generally believed that Schlatter died alone in 1897. It was reported that his skeleton was found lying next to the mysterious copper wand on a lonely hillside in New Mexico.

Interestingly, there was another cosmic cobbler who became known in Colorado, and it wasn't because he claimed to be the Holy Ghost. Ghost hunting and capturing paranormal phenomena on film was what this cosmic cobbler was all about. A.K. Cutting's lifelong fascination with the occult began when he witnessed his father, a well-known American journalist, abducted and then murdered by the Mexican militia in El Paso, Texas. In 1890, Cutting landed in Colorado City, where the young man apprenticed in a cobbler's shop and eventually became a master craftsman. After the owner retired, Cutting bought the shoe shop, added a photography studio and began developing his own photos. Cutting also spent many hours pouring over scientific and metaphysical periodicals. Eventually, the cobbler accepted an eastern theory that all living things had an astral body counterpart. Despite his new beliefs, the scientist was determined to find proof of the paranormal. One day, he happened upon an astonishing article published by the Russian Technical Society that detailed a new kind of photography technique using electric current called an Electrograph and suddenly had a flash of inspiration. At the hardware store, he ordered special film plates and chemicals to be sent from the Kodak Company in New York. Two weeks later, Mr. Cutting was at the train station picking up the supplies when he spotted the perfect subject for his new experiment. Railroad brakeman Joseph Murphy had just rolled into town after an unfortunate accident had severed his right hand. Murphy was understandably suspicious when Cutting asked to photograph the mutilation but agreed to the weird experiment when the cosmic cobbler offered ten bucks for his trouble.

Before entering the dark room, Cutting asked Murphy to concentrate on his missing hand. He then placed Murphy's arm on a highly sensitized piece of photography paper and held it there for five minutes. Cutting held his breath as the minutes ticked by and then screamed with excitement

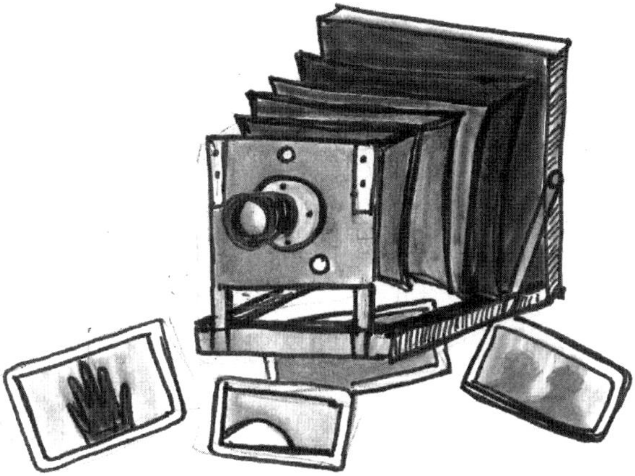

when the image of the missing hand was clearly revealed on the photo paper. Cutting secretly repeated the experiment several more times and even convinced the city street commissioner to cooperate with the strange experiment. On March 4, 1906, A.K. Cutting made national news when the *Colorado Springs Gazette* reported about the visionary man's experiment. The headlines read:

PHOTOGRAPHS ASTRAL HAND
STRANGE EXPERIMENT PERFORMED BY
A.K. CUTTING
MISSING ARM OF STREET
COMMISSONER MYLES IS REPRODUCED
ON KODAK FILM

Cutting worked tirelessly photographing phantom images but never gained serious attention for his lifelong commitment to what he called "astral photography." However, the cosmic cobbler might be happy to know that his high-voltage electro-photography was perfected in 1939 when Russian electrical engineer Semyon Kirlian and his wife, Valentina, invented a new technique they called "Kirlian photography." The couple placed unexposed film on top of a metal discharge plate and then placed a leaf onto the film. A high voltage of current was sent to the plate, creating an exposure, and a corona or aura of the leaf was captured on the film. The couple hoped to use the technique to diagnose illnesses and published a paper about their findings in 1961. In 1970, the bestselling book *Psychic Discoveries Beyond the Iron Curtain* was published, and knowledge about Kirlian photography became widespread. So the next time you happen to be in Colorado Springs for the country's largest psychic fair, step on up to the Kirlian photography booth and have your aura photographed. The unusual photographs make wonderful souvenirs and are much more practical than buying a foam cowboy hat.

For more information about A.K. Cutting's photography lab in Old Colorado City, contact Colorado Ghost Tours at 719-685-2409 or visit their website at www.coloradoghosttours.net.

Chapter 9

Ancient Secrets

As we acquire more knowledge, things do not become more comprehensible but more mysterious.
—Albert Schweitzer

Colorado is well known for its ancient mysteries. In the southern region of the state, the archeological dwellings of Mesa Verde and Chimney Rock are timeless treasures to behold. Archaic hieroglyphics are painted and carved into the rock cliffs in Picket Wire Canyon at the Comanche Grasslands. Outside the town of Springfield is the mystifying Crack Cave. At the crack of dawn, on both the spring and autumnal equinoxes, sunlight strikes through the narrow cave entrance to briefly illuminate an ancient carving of the sun. Some archeologists believe that the prehistoric stone calendar was left by Celtic wayfarers more than two thousand years ago. Many of these mysterious places are associated with well-worn legends. One such place is the Great Sand Dunes National Park, located in the notoriously mysterious San Luis Valley. One legend about the geographic wonder states that you can hear the sands singing songs as the dunes shift in the gentle breeze. Another old story holds that the immemorial dunes are inhabited by ghostly web-footed horses. The American Indians believed that Spirit Lake was haunted by their ancestors. Long ago, Cheyenne and Arapaho Indians attacked a village of Ute Indians. Upon seeing their enemies approach, the Ute warriors put the women and children on rafts and pushed them away from the shore, hoping to protect them from harm. However, a big storm came up and overturned the rafts, and the Ute warriors watched in agony as their helpless loved ones drowned right before their eyes. Spirit Lake is now known as Grand Lake, and local lore holds that the blue mists over the waters are the long-lost souls of the Indians who died in the tragedy.

The greatest mystery of Grand Lake was uncovered when the *Denver Post* announced an amazing discovery with enticing headlines that read, "FREAKISH ROCK FOUND IN COLORADO IS RELIC OF PRE-GLACIAL PERIOD" on December 31, 1922. The sixty-six pound, kidney-shaped, blue granite rock was unearthed by a Granby rancher who was widening a water canal at his home near Grand Lake. The odd-looking relic, christened the Granby Idol, was carved with ancient hieroglyphics, and the top was carved to look like an old man's face. Scientists noted that the flat nose of the ancient relic indicated that it could have possibly been carved at a time predating the Aztecs.

However, the most profound discovery in Colorado was never technically classified, and that fact likely doomed it to remain a mystery for all eternity. On December 20, 1870, the *Rocky Mountain News* flashed an intriguing headline that simply read, "INDIAN GHOST."

For months, folks in Las Animas were talking about a mysterious stranger seen in the region. The enigma was described as an American Indian with luminous white skin who wore a weird costume made from an unknown metallic fabric. The first to report the shimmering stranger was the Bransford family. Time and again, old man Bransford would wake in the middle of the night to hear tapping and scratching on his bedroom ceiling. What was especially unnerving was the fact that the rancher's four watchdogs were so frightened that they would scamper under his bed whenever the haunting phenomena occurred. Each time the noise woke him up, it seemed to last longer and was louder than the time before. When the old man got his gun and searched the premises, nothing was ever found. One night, Mr. Branford's twenty-year-old son was awakened by the odd noise and saw the luminous stranger staring at him from his bedroom doorway. The figure gestured for the rancher's son to follow, and he obeyed as if he were entranced. Moments later, the young man snapped out of the spell and found himself standing in the middle of his yard. The ethereal night stalker was nowhere in sight—it was a big relief, especially since the bewildered man was wearing nothing but his birthday suit. Finally, authorities in Denver sent agents to investigate the strange happenings surrounding the farming community of Las Animas.

The research team stayed at the Bransford ranch and witnessed bizarre phenomena the very first night of the investigation. While the men were sitting around the fireplace, two logs rose out of the flames and danced around each other like they were doing the Mambo. Several times, the leaping logs twirled top over bottom, apparently performing summersaults for the reporters' amusement. Suddenly, the blazing wood shot up the chimney like a bolt of lightning. The astonished guests ran outside to see the logs laying about thirty feet from the house and poured water over them to extinguish the flames. The next morning, the mysterious dancing logs had disappeared. However, a nearby pile of rocks was smoking like a chimney. The *Rocky Mountain News* reported:

> *On the garden of Mr. Bransford are two piles or mounds of stone. Though one of these mounds issues constantly two small columns of smoke. Furthermore, the ground for fifty feet in the neighborhood sounds hollow and gives one the feeling of walking on the deck of a ship.*

The investigators thoroughly searched the rock piles but didn't find a thing. The reporters then dug ten feet underground and found nothing but an ancient stone pedestal made for grinding grain.

The last man to be interviewed was Juan Vasquez, who lived just a half mile east of the Bransford ranch. Several months earlier, Mr. Vasquez had been digging a new foundation on his property one morning when he struck something hard with the spade. The rancher tried to dig out the stubborn rock, but it was in too deep. Vasquez tilted his sombrero to shield his eyes and then proceeded to work the lump out of the bedrock with just a hand tool. After slaving away in the hot sun for hours, the rancher finally pulled the heavy rock from the earth just before lunchtime. After examining the treasure, Juan almost choked on his taco when he suddenly realized that he was holding a gigantic human skull! The dense cranium was more than twice the size of that of the average human, and the eye sockets alone were the size of tortillas! Needless to say, Juan was stunned by the bizarre discovery. The sheep farmer was acutely aware that he had just unearthed a miraculous wonder and gingerly placed the treasure in his wheelbarrow. However, once the bone touched the surface, it crumbled to dust. Juan was flabbergasted, and he knew that his buddies would never believe the wild story, so he dug further and found more pieces of the odd, clay-colored bones. Juan worked feverishly for weeks to recover the curious fossils and eventually unearthed three gigantic human skeletons. Unfortunately, most of the bones turned to powder as soon as they were exposed to the air. Luckily, Juan was able to salvage a few bones that he hauled in his wagon to the only authority in the region. When Trinidad's distinguished Dr.

Boshoar examined the gigantic bones, he too was stumped by the mystery and was quoted in the newspaper as saying, "The bones are much larger than those of any man living today and must belong to a race of giants."

Nothing more was ever reported about the mysteries in Las Animas County, and so explanations about the shimmering night stalker, dancing logs, smoldering rocks and gigantic human bones will likely never be known. Alas, the answers to yet another spectacular Colorado mystery have been lost to the sands of time.

Chapter 10

Rags to Riches

Money often costs too much.
—Ralph Waldo Emerson

There are several well-worn rags-to-riches tales that best exemplified the prosperous Colorado gold rush era. One centers on the handsome miner-turned-mega-millionaire Winfield Scott Stratton, who finally hit pay dirt in Victor after prospecting for nearly twenty years. After making his fortune, Stratton made good on his promise to care for the indigent, becoming one of the most famous philanthropists in Colorado history. One typical example of Stratton's generosity was when he bought bicycles for every cleaning woman in Colorado Springs because he had overheard his maid complaining about walking to work. But not everyone who struck it rich during those golden years died fat and happy. Perhaps the most famous of these unfortunate tales revolves around a down-and-out miner named Robert "Crazy Bob" Womack, who finally struck gold in Poverty Gulch and inadvertently started the Pikes Peak gold rush. It truly was an amazing rag-to-riches story until Crazy Bob traded the mining claim for some quick cash and a case of whiskey. Eight years later, Crazy Bob died in the county poor house without a pot to pee in and turned his life story into a regrettable rags-to-riches-to-rags-again tale. Another such story is that of a poor little country girl who would one day become the silver queen of the West. Her fairy-tale wedding would be attended by celebrated dignitaries, and her dress would cost more than what any average man would earn in his lifetime. This fair lady had a classic beauty that could launch a thousand ships, and songs were written about her fabled charms. Yet this once celebrated woman died alone in abject poverty nearly half a century after her rise to fame and fortune. Even to this day, folks in Leadville swear that you can still hear the gentle winds whisper, "Whatever happened to Baby Doe?"

Elizabeth McCourt was born into a large Irish Catholic family in Oshkosh, Wisconsin. Being one of eleven children fostered a competitive edge in young Lizzie, who grew to be an accomplished athlete. As a teenager, she won the coveted first-place cup in a local ice-skating championship but was disqualified after judges discovered she was a cheat. The contest was for men only, but that didn't stop Lizzie. In fact, few things ever did, especially Harvey Doe's parents, who believed that the McCourt clan was socially beneath them. Elizabeth endured a secret courtship with Harvey for several years until they were finally married in 1877. While the wedding bells were still ringing in their ears, the newlyweds hitched their wagon to a star and headed to the land of milk and honey. Harvey Doe's uncle had a mining job waiting for him in the boomtown of Black Hawk. Unfortunately, their happiness was short lived. Harvey turned out to be a spoiled mama's boy who shirked all his responsibilities, including his wife. Harvey was so drunk when Lizzie gave birth that he didn't realize their baby was stillborn until the next day. Lo and behold, after three miserable years of matrimony, Elizabeth left Harvey and implied that the only good thing that came out of their union was the endearing nickname he gave her—Baby Doe.

Baby Doe was as delicate as a little china doll, but what she lacked in stature she more than made up for in courage. Divorce was uncommon in 1880, especially for a young catholic woman, but Baby Doe was determined to leave both the negative stigma and her unhappy life behind. In the mining camp of Leadville, she turned over a new leaf, and she soon made many good friends. The miners were attracted to Baby Doe's beauty and bubbly personality, and the sultry seamstress could have had her choice in men but fell for Horace "H.A.W." Tabor. The tall, dark and handsome millionaire had struggled all his life before making a fortune by grubstaking broken-down miners. The suave playboy was married to his polar opposite—the prim and proper Augusta Tabor—who was growing rather embarrassed by her hubby's philandering ways. Baby Doe was attracted to Tabor's bad-boy reputation, and after meeting the handsome silver-haired fox, she fell head over heels in love. Again, the young woman was determined to get her man and conceded to a secret three-year affair with Tabor until he finally agreed to make her an honest woman. However, Baby Doe underestimated Mrs. Tabor, a formidable foe who wasn't about to leave her marriage without a fight. Augusta proudly announced to the newspapers that she had stood by her husband for many years, bore him a son and helped build his massive empire, and she was not going to give up her man to some shameless, gold-digging hussy! The airing of Mrs. Tabor's dirty linens was the biggest news sensation of the year, and newspapers wrote thrilling headlines about the scandalous love triangle. On October 30, 1885, headlines in a Cincinnati newspaper screamed:

TABOR DIVORCE SUIT
CONSIDERABLE EVIDENCE SHOWING
THE COMPLAINING HUSBAND IN A VERY
BAD LIGHT

However, Augusta's outspoken hostility backfired, and her estranged husband became more determined than ever to dissolve their crumbling relationship. The duped woman was furious when she read the astonishing headlines announcing that her marriage was over. Apparently, H.A.W. and his slick attorney pulled a fast one by procuring an illegal divorce in Durango, but Augusta didn't discover the deception until it was already too late. The heartbreaking scandal was particularly painful when the unbelievable news was followed by Horace and Baby Doe's shocking wedding announcement. The opulent shindig was held at the Willard Hotel in Washington, D.C., and was considered to be the social event of a lifetime. The bride wore a stunning $7,000 white satin brocade wedding gown trimmed in crystal sequins and marabou, and her diamond necklace had once graced the neck of Queen Isabelle of Spain. President Chester A. Arthur was even there to kiss the bride, and everyone who was anyone was invited to the grand affair. But the Washington wives went on the warpath against the home-wrecking harlot and refused to attend the grand soiree, so their husbands attended alone. Needless to say, half of the crystal champagne flutes were never toasted, and there was plenty of elbowroom on the dance floor. Sadly, it would not be the last time that Baby Doe would be snubbed by the fat cats of high society.

The Tabors spared no expense pampering their first born, whose christening gown alone cost a whopping $15,000 dollars. Another daughter was born just a few years later, and Baby Doe delighted in showing off their growing brood. Oshkosh welcomed the Tabors with open arms, and Baby Doe was overjoyed when a special homecoming parade was held in their honor. For one glorious decade, Baby Doe lived the life of Cinderella, with her handsome prince, a glorious castle in Denver, several carriages and various servants who attended to her every whim. Yet the old battle axes of Denver's Capitol Hill still refused to acknowledge Baby Doe. The blue bloods became especially angered after the Tabors disgraced the neighborhood with offensive artwork on their front lawn. When Baby Doe heard complaints about the naked bronze goddesses, she ordered her tailor to fashion the statues with sexy lingerie! The Tabors relished their extravagant lifestyle and lived high on the hog while their employed miners were paid only three measly dollars a day. Apparently, Baby Doe and Horace forgot what it was like to be poor, and that is why their fall from grace was so ironic. It's hard to believe, but after the silver market suddenly went belly up, the Tabors were flat broke in no time at all. Anyone who ever doubted Baby Doe's love for Horace was fooled when she remained true to her love throughout the embarrassing scandal. Most of their so-called friends shamelessly turned their backs, and only a few remained loyal. One of them allowed the Tabors to live at Denver's Windsor Hotel, and Horace was humbled to secure a job as a postmaster.

Upon hearing about her ex-husband's grave misfortune, Augusta undoubtedly reveled with comforting thoughts of sweet revenge. The shrewd businesswoman never forgot her thrifty ways and had wisely invested her meager divorce settlement, turning it into a fortune. Unlike her freewheeling ex-husband, Augusta's frugal spending afforded her a comfortable retirement. Upon her death, she left an honorable legacy for her children and was well regarded for her generous philanthropy. However, Baby

Doe's life took an entirely different course. Over the years, she became estranged from friends, her adult children, parents and siblings. The middle-aged woman became especially bitter after Horace died, as she was all alone in the world. Just when the desperate woman thought she could no longer bare the humiliation, she found strength in remembering her husband's ominous dying words: "Hold on to the Matchless Mine, Baby Doe. It will make you a rich woman again one day."

After Horace's funeral, Baby Doe, although poor as a church mouse, managed to scavenge enough money to buy a one-way ticket back to her old stomping grounds. When Baby Doe got to Leadville, she moved into an abandoned shack next to the deserted Matchless Mine. Residents would see Baby Doe wander into town every now and again, but most kept their distance from the reclusive woman. In the winter months, Baby Doe staved off the bitter cold by wrapping her feet in gunnies sacks and lining her ragged clothes with yellowed newspaper. Over the years, a few concerned neighbors left scraps of food and buckets of coal on her doorstep. Some of these kind-hearted souls later recounted how Baby Doe returned to her devout Catholic roots. Baby Doe had plenty of time for reflection, outliving her beloved husband by thirty-five long years. In March 1935, a neighbor lady discovered Baby Doe frozen to death on the floor of her shack, with her arms mysteriously outstretched in the shape of a cross. Strangely, the old woman appeared much younger than her eighty-one years.

Adding to the mystery was the peaceful smile and eerie look of tranquility frozen on the dead woman's placid face. Perhaps just before death, Baby Doe remembered her husband's ominous dying words and realized that the Matchless Mine had made her a rich woman again after all.

The greatest pride of Leadville is its museums. Smart tourists plan ahead and visit the museums from Memorial Day through Labor Day. The Matchless Mine and Baby Doe Museum is one of the places you will really want to see. 719-486-1229.

Chapter 11

Shameless Showdowns

Courage is being scared to death but saddling up anyway.
—John Wayne

Several historical gunfights in Colorado were just like what you see in old spaghetti westerns, with handsome good guys in white cowboy hats standing off against tobacco-spitting outlaws. The dramatic shoot-outs were usually over money, drinking, gambling or women. One unbelievable showdown was reminiscent of a Shakespearean tragedy, but the only reminder of the calamity is a lone tombstone just outside a long-forgotten ghost town. The story holds that in the spring of 1879, the sheriff was at his wit's end when a stagecoach robber got away with several robberies just outside town. The townsfolk blamed the sheriff, who in turn took his frustration out on the stage line. After several weeks of bickering, the lawman decided to put an end to the blame game once and for all. When the next scheduled stage was about to arrive in Balltown, the sheriff ambushed the thief and caught him by surprise. Bullets ricocheted off the cliffs like lightning bolts and echoed through the canyon like deafening thunder. The robber tried to flee, but the lawman hotly pursued and shot him dead. The passengers cheered with great relief, as the heroic good guy had saved the day, but the celebration was short lived. When the lawman pulled the cowboy hat off the villain, long blonde hair tumbled out, revealing that he was actually a she. The passengers were aghast at the horrific discovery, but the sheriff just snickered and warned that outlaws would be equally dealt with regardless of gender. However, the lawman soon changed his tune when the outlaw's mask was removed. The sheriff sat in stunned silence for a moment and then cried like a baby after realizing he'd just killed his own wife! The guilt was so unbearable that he shamefully buried the mother of his children on the very spot where he killed her. Perhaps the lawman was too embarrassed to bury the outlaw in the family plot, but at least he had the decency to erect the lonesome tombstone, which reads:

MY WIFE
JANE KIRKHAM
DIED MARCH 7, 1879
AGE 38 YEARS, 3 MONTHS AND 7 DAYS

The Buena Vista Historical Society confirms that the legend is true, although the details are somewhat sketchy.

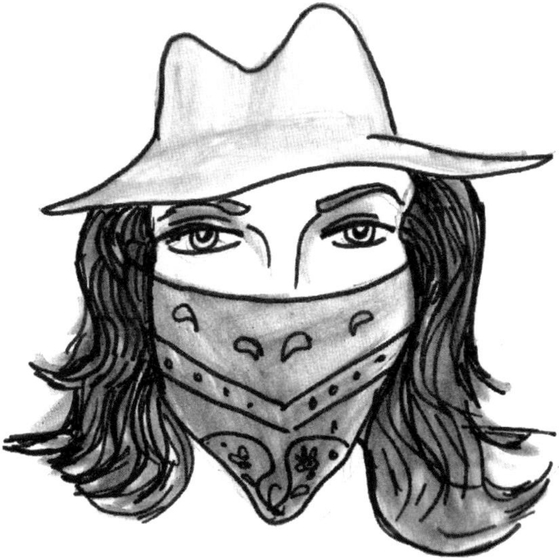

The other version of the story is that it was actually the stagecoach driver who killed the sheriff's bandit wife.

Another infamous showdown involved two colorful characters well known in the Tenderloin district of Denver. The dramatic duel was the talk of the town back in 1877—not for the tears shed or blood spilled but because it occurred between two popular, wealthy women. Madam Mattie Silks and her archrival, the up-and-coming Kate Fulton, were both prosperous businesswomen on Denver's Market Street. On this infamous city block, a man could have a date with a pretty gal—but it would cost him a pretty penny, especially at Madam Mattie's. The luxurious brothel was known as the House of Mirrors, and it was the finest bordello around, bar none. Kate Fulton was envious of the older woman's high-flouting clientele, and in turn, Mattie was jealous of Kate's youthful charms. The harlots made no secret about the bad blood between them, and tensions mounted as the years wore on. One day, Mattie put her money where her mouth was by sponsoring her boyfriend in a footrace against Kate's champion. The rules were simple: the winner would take all, and the loser would leave town. Mattie's beau, wearing star-spangled athletic shorts over bright pink tights, came in first place, but just by a nose hair. Kate immediately cried foul play. The spoiled loser threw a temper tantrum and demanded a rematch. Mattie flatly refused, pocketed the winnings and promptly invited the crowd to a victory party. Heated words were exchanged, and in a matter of seconds, a bloody battle ensued. Like any good catfight, there was a great deal of scratching and biting until Kate broke a fingernail and screamed, "Time Out!" Once the fur stopped flying, an amused spectator suggested a duel, and the maddened madams gladly agreed. The next day, the vexed vixens were to square off at sundown, but when both women arrived three sheets to the wind, spectators assumed they were stonewalling. Before the referee finished going through the rules, Madame Kate spilled her beer and accidently sent a stray bullet into a tree. Mattie promptly threw off her floppy hat and then fired with fierce precision. Her bullet hit…but not the target she had aimed for. At least Mattie's boyfriend wasn't badly hurt when his neck was grazed by the bullet. Perhaps something good came out of the embarrassing fiasco, because after two near misses, the harried harlots threw down their weapons and called a truce.

Several gun duels were fought on the dusty streets of Durango, and a couple even made national headlines. Perhaps the oddest was between two of the unlikeliest gunslingers: newspapermen. Back in 1903, the chief editor of the *Democrat* became furious when one of his writers became a union activist. For several weeks, the two journalists publically jabbed each other with insidious barbs. Finally, it was agreed that a showdown on Durango's infamous Main Street would be the only way to end their venomous dispute. In Portland, headlines in the May 20, 1903 issue of the *Oregonian* read:

EDITORS FIGHT DUEL
THIRTEEN SHOTS ARE FIRED, BUT NEITHER IS HURT
MEET ON MAIN STREET OF THE CITY
SHOOTING THE OUTCOME OF A FIGHT AGAINST UNION PRINTERS AND CAUSTIC PERSONAL REFERENCES OF WRITERS TO EACH OTHER

With so many bullets flying, it begs the question of which showdown was most appalling. Historians likely agree that it was the infamous battle in which two good guys fought until death. Sheriff Thompson was known as the salt of the earth. At six foot four, the handsome, broad-shouldered lawman cut an intimidating image. Thompson's quest for justice was daunting in the lawless hellhole of Durango, so he was forced to rule with an iron fist and stick to the books as far as following the rules was concerned. The dutiful sheriff loved strong drink but detested gambling and made no bones about his quest to eliminate the illegal activity. Thompson was especially outraged to learn that a hushed gambling operation thrived at the El Moro Saloon, which was co-owned by Marshal Jesse Stansel, who had the audacity to run his office out of the illegal establishment. When the sheriff demanded that the operation be shut down, the deputy marshal flatly refused. Sheriff Thompson was hot under the collar and fired the first shot. Flying bullets zigzagged down Main Street, and flabbergasted bystanders ran for cover. After the lawmen ran out of bullets, they preceded to pistol whip each other until they both hit the ground. As the brilliant sunset cast a golden hue over the mountains, the streets of Durango ran red with blood. Sadly, two good men died in the horrific tragedy. Sheriff Thompson was pronounced dead at the hospital, as was an innocent bystander who just happened to be at the wrong place at the wrong time. News of the wicked showdown spread all across the country. In San Jose, California, headlines in the January 10, 1906 edition of the *Evening News* reported: "SHERIFF KILLED IN STREET DUEL."

When all was said and done, the "Teflon Marshal" miraculously recovered from his multiple wounds. The townsfolk were flabbergasted when the dirty dog walked away from the double homicide when charges didn't stick. Thankfully, the marshal was smart enough to know he was no longer welcome in Durango.

For more information on historical Chaffee County, please visit the Buena Vista Museum or call the Buena Vista Historical Society at 719-293-1700.

For more information about Durango's interesting history, a visit to the Animas Museum, operated by the La Plata Historical Society, is a must see. For more information, please visit www.animasmuseum.org or call 970-259-2402.

Chapter 12

Beer for an Ear

Death and vulgarity are the only two facts in the nineteenth century that one cannot explain away.
—Oscar Wilde

Several notorious outlaws called Colorado home for a spell. Clay Allison hung his holster in Las Animas, while Butch Cassidy's gang was holed up at Brown's Park for a time. Notorious assassinator Bob Ford owned a gambling hall in Creed until he was murdered in the same cowardly fashion in which he killed Jesse James. Gentleman gambler Doc Holiday died in a Glenwood Springs tuberculosis hospital. His last words were said to have been, "This is funny," no doubt because he died with his boots off. However, there is one forgotten gunslinger that became infamous during his time in Colorado. After Mark Twain met Captain Jack Slade, he wrote that the notorious frontiersman was more feared than God himself. Old-timers used to say that Slade possessed a kind spirit when he was sober but warned about the wild man when in his cups. It was said that Slade killed well over twenty-six men during his short life. However, his main claim to fame was a watch fob that he fashioned from the stiff organ of a former foe—but more on that delicate subject later in the story.

Long before Jack Slade ever developed a taste for sin and liquor, he was already a lost cause. The gunslinger killed his first victim in an Illinois schoolyard when he was just knee-high to a grasshopper. His frustrated parents sent him away to mend his wicked ways, and he eventually joined the Mexican War. Just a few years later, the fearless soldier was promoted to captain and met his better half, Virginia Dale. Virginia and Jack dearly loved each other because he saved her from an insufferable life of prostitution, and she saved him from himself. No doubt the odd-looking couple turned a few heads whenever they walked by. Virginia was a beautiful, statuesque woman with the patience of a saint. Jack, on the other hand, was a scrappy little man who was well known for his hot temper. Jack and Virginia were both gifted sharpshooters, skilled horseback riders and ambitious to beat the band. Not long after they were married, the lovebirds flew the coop and landed in the Colorado territory. Captain Slade got a job with the Overland Stage Company and worked his way up to district manager. His biggest concern was a small, poorly managed stage stop on the border of Nebraska in a rambunctious town called Julesburg.

It's been said that only the wicked lived in Julesburg during the early days. The town was home to many social misfits, including Jules Beni, a deceitful French Canadian who helped build the Overland Stage stop. The rotund Frenchman was one of the first residents in the hub of Overland, and so no one argued when he renamed the town Julesburg, after himself. Beni was eventually fired from the stage company due to his poor management and did not like meeting his new replacement, the scrawny, pencil-necked Jack Slade. The two men took to each other like oil does to water, and tensions mounted, especially after several Overland horses were stolen from the stage stop. Jack Slade inadvertently discovered the missing horses on Beni's ranch and had no problems confiscating his employer's property. As Slade rode off with the stolen horses in tow, Beni fired a few bullets after him, warning that his days were numbered.

A few months later, in the spring of 1860, Jack Slade rode into Julesburg dead tired after working the trail. When Slade opened the door to the general store, Jules Beni ambushed him from behind the counter, shooting six bullets, and Jack fell to the floor. Still not satisfied with the victory, Beni blasted two more rounds from a double-barreled shotgun just for good measure. Elated with the triumph, Beni instructed two awestruck bystanders to let Jack bleed dry before burying him down by the river. As Beni walked out the door, Jack Slade weakly croaked the infamous dying words, "I will live long enough to see your ear on my watch chain." The fat Frenchman laughed wickedly at the absurd threat, but before he could make his escape, the stage thundered into Julesburg with the head honcho of the Overland Company on board. The superintendent bellowed that Beni would be executed on the spot for the atrocity committed against Jack Slade, and a hurried makeshift scaffolding was constructed just for the special occasion. Strange enough, the Frenchman's heavy girth kept snapping the weak noose, and after three unsuccessful attempts, the coward got off scot-free with the promise that he would never return to Julesburg.

Months later, word got around the grapevine that Slade had miraculously survived and was seeking revenge. But Beni didn't believe the absurd rumors. One fateful day, Beni looked up from a game of poker to see a cocked pistol in his face. The fat Frenchman looked as if he'd seen a ghost when he realized that Jack Slade was actually alive. Slade delighted in tying his arch nemesis to a nearby fencepost and spent the afternoon joyously firing pot shots just to watch the Frenchman squirm. Finally, Slade cut off Beni's ears and then put a bullet between his eyes. He ceremoniously nailed one plump ear to the fencepost as a warning to other possible troublemakers and then fashioned the other into an unusual watch fob, which he proudly sported everywhere he went. Jack Slade eventually surrendered to authorities in Fort Laramie and pleaded his case. His honesty paid off, and he was released from custody and absolved of all charges. Jack and his wife then moved to a new stagecoach station, which Jack sentimentally named Virginia Dale, near present-day Greely. Not long after, it was implied that the couple was harboring fugitives at their hillside hacienda and that it had become a known robber's roost. So the Slades moved once again, this time to Virginia City, Montana, where Jack built a lovely little rock cottage for his devoted wife. However, paradise was soon lost when, in 1864, Jack went on yet another wild drinking spree, tore up the town and attempted to kidnap the judge. A group of angry vigilantes had had enough of Slade's drunken shenanigans and held a necktie party, making the little rascal the guest of honor. Legend holds that Virginia couldn't bear being separated from her beloved husband and paid a small fortune to have Jack's corpse sealed in a custom zinc-lined coffin. Virginia spread a feather mattress over the casket and happily slept with her deceased hubby until the putrid odor grew unbearable. She finally hired a stagecoach, tied Jack's coffin to the top and went all the way to Salt Lake City to bury him because she didn't want Jack buried in the wicked land where he was murdered.

Jack Slade will always be remembered in Colorado for his dogged revenge and for sporting his gruesome trophy wherever he went. Years later, the *Colorado Springs Gazette* featured an amusing article on November 27, 1904, with the headline, "RUFFIAN USED HUMAN EAR AS BEER CHECK IN EARLY DAYS." The article detailed how a cowboy walked into a Colorado City saloon boasting that he was mighty thirsty and wanted to trade "a beer for an ear." The cowboy then threw down the

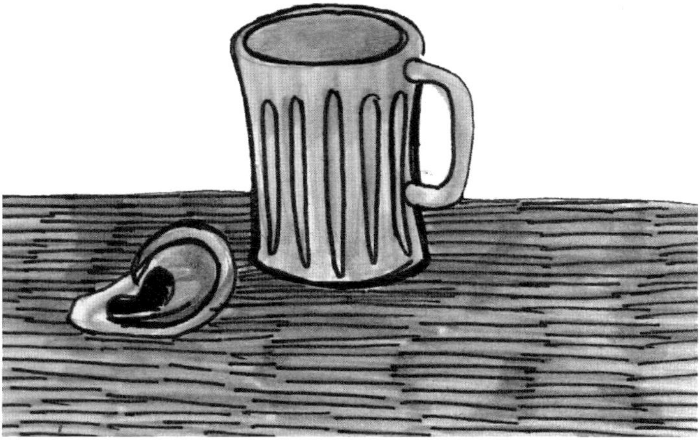

blackened, shriveled organ on the bar top for payment. No doubt it was Jack Slade, and he must have roared with laughter after asking the bartender to make change for the gruesome trophy.

Colorado City was incorporated as Colorado Springs and is now referred to as Old Colorado City. For more information, please visit the Old Colorado City Historical Society and museum or call 719-636-1225.

Chapter 13

Vile Vigilantes

Cowards die many times before their deaths; the valiant never taste of death but once.
—William Shakespeare

The job of maintaining order on the turbulent western frontier was no easy task, and only the savviest of lawmen survived. Resources were limited in the early days, so the most important asset a lawman could have was loyal friends on his side. Notions toward the judicial system could easily sour overnight, and not all authority figures were respected. Vigilante gangs began popping up all over the territory, and the most notorious of all was known as the Committee for Safety. This gang of renegade ranchers used the mills along Chalk Creek as secret headquarters where they tortured and murdered their enemies. The vigilantes waged wars against local landowners over water rights and issued "coffin notices" to those who did not comply.

Tensions mounted when prominent English rancher George Harrington refused association with the committee and holed up in his ranch house. One dark, stormy night, thirty masked gunmen rode to the Harrington homestead, stacked firewood around his house and held a bonfire in the Englishman's honor. Tragically, Harrington was shot in the back for attempting to put out the flames and thus became the first victim of the infamous Lake County War. Several people were victimized during the yearlong feud, including a well-known district court judge who paid a high price for his heroic call of duty.

You could say that Judge Elias Dyer was in dire straights when the Lake County War erupted, as he alone had to tow the line of justice. Dyer was the son of a popular pioneer preacher, but not everyone acknowledged his authority or respected his heritage. In February 1875, the committee rode to the county seat in Granite with trumped-up charges against an associate of Dyer's, but the judge refused to cooperate, so they held him hostage. Finally, after three days, Judge Dyer agreed to leave the county but then immediately went tattling to Governor Jenkins. The bigwigs on Capitol Hill failed to recognize the dire emergency and refused to enact marshal law but sent an agent to investigate the judge's claims. A week later, an officer reported that everything was hunky-dory in Lake County, and the judge nervously returned to the bench. Judge Dyer stuck to his guns and issued sixteen warrants to various members of the vigilante gang on charges ranging from harassment to murder. But Sheriff Dobbins was no dummy, and he refused to serve the summons. The judge dismissed the charges when nobody showed up for court. Yet Judge Dyer's act of mercy was too little too late because the very next morning, dozens of angry committee members surrounded the courthouse. The judge dismissed proceedings for the day but stubbornly refused to leave the courthouse. That night, Dyer sat alone and watched from the lofty windows as the hostile ranchers burned an effigy in his honor. The scorned judge wrote a heartfelt letter to his father that was later published in the newspaper. It read:

> *Granite, July 3, 1875. I don't know that the sun will ever rise or set for me again, but I trust in God and his mercy. At 8 o'clock, I sit in court. The mob has me under guard. There is no cowardice in me, father. I am worthy of you in this respect. I am, in this one respect, like him who died for us all: I die if I must, for law, order and principal; and too I stand alone.*

The next morning, several angry cowboys armed to the teeth rushed up the back staircase and burst into the courtroom. One threw a noose on the lawman's desk while the others hooted with laughter. Angry words were exchanged, and seven shots rang out. When the smoke cleared the air, thirty-nine-year-old Judge Dyer was dead. Although there were several witnesses, they all had short memories, and murder charges were never brought against the vile villains. Three years later, the judge's grave was moved to the family plot in Castle Rock, and brave Judge Dyer was given a befitting headstone, which reads in part:

A VICTIM OF THE MURDEROUS MOB
RULING IN LAKE COUNTY

One peculiar story shared around the water trough was published on November 19, 1904, when the *Denver Post* headlined, "SHERIFF SAYS MUTILATORS GOT THE WRONG MAN."

Two respectable doctors volunteering for civic duty on election night were suddenly kidnapped from city hall by a raging mob of lunatics. At the Montrose County jail, the vigilantes forced the physicians to perform an impromptu sex-change operation on a prisoner being held on molestation charges. It wasn't until after the abrupt surgery that the mutilators discovered that they had accidentally plucked the wrong rooster. Unfortunately, the horrific case of mistaken identity didn't keep folks from wanting more of the same kind of vigilante justice. Just three weeks later, the *Denver Post* published an article from a citizen suggesting that the Montrose vigilantes pluck another vile prisoner being held in Grand Junction.

The most extraordinary case of vile vigilantes still amazes Colorado historians. The story began when ten-year-old Mary Rose was happily adopted by a couple who owned a sprawling ranch outside Ouray. The child 's hope was soon dashed when she realized that the Cuddingtons only adopted her for slave labor. Mary Rose was forced to play nursemaid to the couple's one-year-old son and was expected to care for their coming baby as well. Mrs. Cuddington was heavy with child, and little Mary was forced to do all the household chores and wasn't allowed friends or schooling. Over time, neighbors noticed that the happy little girl had grown sullen and was often covered with bruises. The Cuddingtons blamed the girl's neglected appearance on her just being a rough-and-tumble tomboy. Then, one cold day in January 1884, a hunter found the scantily clad child crawling from a haystack near the Cuddington ranch. Mary Rose's bare feet were frost bitten, so he kindly carried her home. Mrs. Cuddington cursed that it served the child right for running away in the first place. A few days later, concerned neighbors went to check on the youngster and were stunned to learn that Mary Rose had died after falling down the stairs. The suspicious sheriff ordered Mary's grave at the Cuddington ranch to be exhumed. As expected, the coroner confirmed the murder suspicion, and the Cuddingtons were promptly arrested. Late that night, the couple was abducted when the jailer conveniently looked the other way. An angry mob dragged the belligerent prisoners through the dark streets of Ouray by the eerily flickering flames of torchlight until the hoi polloi finally reached the edge of town. A rope was thrown over the ridgepole of an abandoned cabin while Mr. Cuddington made a last-ditch effort to proclaim his innocence. The hangman snickered wickedly at the rancher's sniveling pleas and slid the noose even tighter around his scrawny neck. Mr. Cuddington feverishly prayed aloud to all the saints in heaven but choked on his dying words when he was jerked to Jesus. Mrs. Cuddington belted out a bloodcurdling scream as she watched her husband violently convulse above the raging mob. A readied rope was then thrown over the lofty branch of a cottonwood tree, and the unbridled crowd cheered upon seeing that there would be an encore performance. The young mother cried for the sake of her little boy at home and for the life of her unborn child, but her horrific cries fell on deaf ears. Mrs. Cuddington screamed in terror when the hangman's noose was slipped over her head and the executioner hissed that it was time for the child killer to die. A split second later, the pregnant woman was sent kicking above the roaring crowd until she slowly strangled to death on the hemp necklace. News of the vigilantes' wicked execution quickly spread across the country, and by and large, people were aghast about the blood spilled in Ouray. The *New Haven Register* blasted the following headlines:

RELENTLESSS REVENGERS LYNCHING A MAN AND HIS WIFE
VIGILANTES IN REVENGE FOR A POOR GIRL WHO HAD BEEN HORRIBLY MALTREATED
CURSES AND PRAYERS INTERMINGLED

Newspapers reported how the gruesome corpses of the ranching couple were displayed for public viewing. One story told of how Mrs. Cuddington's eyes bulged from her head and how Mr. Cuddington's withered tongue hung from his blood-foamed mouth. No doubt the horrific details sold a lot of newspapers, and folks came from all around the country just to take a gander. The scornful townsfolk agreed that the Cuddingtons got their just rewards and refused to allow them to be buried in the city cemetery, so the despicable couple was interred at their ranch. Little Mary Rose was taken to Denver, where she was at least given a decent Christian burial. The vile vigilantes were never arrested for murdering the Cuddingtons; however, nobody in town ever complained about it either.

The ghost town of Granite, once the county seat of Lake County, is now part of Chaffee County.

Chapter 14

Revenge

Revenge is a dish best served cold.
—Dorothy Parker

Every schoolboy knows that revenge is a wild justice, and nowhere was that more true than in the Old West. One infamous tale of wild revenge happened on Christmas Eve 1854. Unsuspecting settlers at Fort Pueblo were celebrating the holiday with Taos Lightning when the Indians came knocking on the door under the innocent guise of wanting to trade furs for fire water. When the drunken soldiers opened the gate, the Indians charged into the fort with raised tomahawks, slaughtering everyone in sight. The Utes and Arapahos were angered by the smallpox epidemic that had been spread by diseased blankets given to them by American soldiers. The Indians got revenge again in 1865, but this time, their weapon of destruction was bacon. When a wagonload of the savory breakfast meat was sent to Fort Halleck, it was hijacked by a party of Indians seeking revenge for the recent massacre at Sand Creek. Tragically, Lieutenant Baker was dragged from the wagon, tied to the wheel, tortured for hours and scalped. When the savage Arapahos discovered that the soldier was still alive, they joyfully wrapped Baker in the bacon, set him on fire and cooked his goose, so to speak. I guess you could joke that Baker couldn't even save his own bacon. As you can imagine, stories of revenge were quite prevalent in Colorado, but the following forgotten tale might surprise you at just how far one person would go to seek it.

When Otis Bush was a baby, he was abandoned by his mother. Rumors were that the child wasn't even the legitimate son of John Bush, but the farmer raised the boy as his own with the mixed blessings of his mother. Mrs. Nancy Bush and her son co-owned a ranch near the farming community of Olathe. Sadly, Otis was often neglected and had to beg for food and hand-me-downs from neighbors. Mrs. Craig took a shine to the neglected boy, who became the apple of her eye. This angered Mrs. Bush, who often accused her neighbor of being a busybody. In mid-December 1917, Mrs. Craig realized that she had not seen little Otis in awhile, so she decided to pay him a visit. Mrs. Bush was dressed in mourning attire when she begrudgingly invited her neighbor inside to shake off the chill. The living room was as neat as a pin, except for one wall that was cluttered with pictures and photographs. A couple of frames were mysteriously draped with a black shawl. Mrs. Bush flatly explained that the photographs were shrouded because she was grieving her missing son and grandson, who she feared were dead. Mrs. Craig suggested they call the sheriff, but this angered Mrs. Bush, who immediately showed her neighbor to the door. The next morning, lawmen went snooping around outside the Bush homestead and found fractured bones in the outdoor fire pit. When the sheriff showed Mrs. Bush the evidence, the old woman just scoffed and said that the bones were likely remnants from slaughtered chickens. A posse went hunting for John Bush and his son, and the bone samples were immediately sent to a Denver crime lab.

Days went by, and no stone was left unturned in Montrose County. When no further evidence was found, the sheriff went back to Mrs. Bush's farm with a search warrant in hand. The lawman didn't beat around the bush when explaining legal procedure. Although Mrs. Bush didn't have much book learnin', she knew the official paper stamped with a shiny golden seal meant trouble. Dozens of volunteers scoured the Bush properties, and their valiant efforts paid off. Hidden behind Mrs. Bush's barn was a pair of blood-spattered women's boots, thirteen empty bottles of lye, a large kettle and the leg bone of an adult male. The windfall of circumstantial evidence was all that was needed to arrest the old woman for murdering her son and grandson. It took fifteen months for the case to finally go to trial, but when it did, the headlines of the *Denver Post* shouted:

PLACED ON TRIAL FOR TWO MURDERS MRS. NANCY BUSH PLACED ON TRIAL FOR KILLING BOTH HER SON AND GRANDSON

The trial began on April Fools' Day, but no one was laughing when Mrs. Bush proclaimed that she was innocent of all charges. After weeks of testimony, she took the stand and finally admitted to killing only her son by using the "I killed him, but he deserved it" defense. When that failed to gain sympathy, Mrs. Bush claimed that she had murdered her son in self-defense, but the jurors didn't buy that lame reason either. After running the gauntlet of excuses, Mrs. Bush finally admitted that she was angry with her son for killing her grandson and simply wanted revenge. The grandmother testified that one night, John got drunk as a monkey and accidently killed Otis and then destroyed the corpse. Later that night, Mrs. Bush crept into her son's bedroom, pounded him with a frying pan, butchered his corpse and used a toy wagon to haul his body parts, chunk by chunk, to a boiling caldron of lye.

After just three hours of deliberation, the jury found the seventy-two-year-old grandmother guilty of murdering her son. She was sentenced to life in the state penitentiary. After the sentence was read aloud, the old woman looked pathetically at the jury and cried, "I just did to my own son what he did to his." Perhaps the old granny was off her rocker and didn't know that revenge is always a dish that is best served cold.

The El Pueblo History Museum, located at 301 North Union Boulevard, is built atop the old fort where the Christmas Eve massacre occurred in 1854. According to local legend, the museum is haunted.

Western museum junkies will enjoy visiting the Museum of the Mountain West in Montrose, which exhibits artifacts from Butch Cassidy's Wild Bunch along with other historical novelties. The museum is located on U.S. 50 East on Miami Road.

Chapter 15

Hellfire and Brimstone

Here lies Charlotte. She was a harlot for fifteen years, but she preserved her virginity a damn good record for this vicinity.
—Cemetery epitaph

Colorado is well known for its nefarious Wild West towns. Oscar Wilde christened Julesburg as the "Wickedest City of the West" because of its rambunctious outlaws. In the mining town of Tin Cup, several lawmen were assassinated by ruffians. The prairie town of Trail City was also notorious for its outlaw activity, but all that remains of its former glory days are crumbling foundations, tumbleweeds and plenty of hungry rattlesnakes. It might be hard to believe that the ghost town was once a desert oasis for the trail-hopping cowboys of Colorado, Kansas, Oklahoma and Texas. The southeastern border town began in 1885 at the crossroads of several cattle trails, and although officially christened Trail City, the hamlet was better known as Cowboy City. The infamous watering hole was the end of the trail for some and the beginning for others. The prairie party town was said to be a young man's fancy, and it was always a great place for a roll in the hay or to wet your whistle, especially since neighboring Kansas was a dry state. Twenty-seven bawdy establishments, including saloons, gambling halls and bordellos, lined the east side of Main Street, with Colorado at the front door and Kansas at the back. The setup was ideal for outlaws on the lam, and the town became a veritable robbers' roost. If a marshal from Kansas happened to show up with a warrant in hand, a cowboy would just two-step over to Colorado, where he was a free man. The hellhole was infamous for its live entertainment, as lusty ladies from the bordellos often rode bareback down Main Street, wearing nothing but a smile!

In 1859, one of the first proper towns established in the territory was christened Colorado City. Originally, the mining hamlet was known as the territorial capital, but that honor was eventually bestowed on Denver, and Colorado City never got over it. Once the railroad came into town, all hell broke loose, and the hub soon became known as a veritable sin city. Lascivious and illegal activities thrived in the red-light district, and lawmen had a tough time maintaining order in the town. Innocent-looking Chinese laundries were actually underground opium dens, and brothels were discreetly advertised as finishing schools or riding academies. The south side of Colorado Avenue was reserved for the numerous bawdy establishments. Since dignified gentlemen would never be caught dead crossing the street, secret tunnels leading to the underworld were used for their discretion. Colorado City was thrown into the national spotlight when famed Temperance League spokeswoman Carrie Nation lectured from the Wycott Opera House. The prohibitionist often raided drinking establishments with hatchet in hand, bashing everything that didn't move. The resolute reformist warned that drunkards were tearing at the social fabric of society and implored townsfolk to vote Colorado City dry. Laws were tightened, and bawdy establishments were fined, but civility remained elusive in the Wild West town. Hostilities escalated when several mysterious fires, which barkeepers immediately blamed on the Temperance League, erupted in the red-light district. During one of the fires, seventy-two-year-old Blanche Burton was sent running from her house with her nightgown afire. Sadly, the hot-to-trot madam died just a few hours later. The infamous harlot was buried on Christmas Eve 1909, and the *Colorado Springs Gazette* featured a story about the life of the hooker with a heart of gold. The headlines proclaimed:

DID MUCH GOOD
MRS. BLANCHE BURTON WAS EVER
READY TO BEFREIND THE POOR
FUNERAL THIS AFTERNOON

Some folks believed that notorious Colorado City madam Laura Bell McDaniel was also victimized by the revengeful teetotalers. The flamboyant redhead was perhaps the most successful madam in Colorado. At one time, the queen of the tenderloin built a veritable empire of sin, with bawdy houses running simultaneously in Colorado City, Cripple Creek and Salida. Laura Bell was well known for her jaw-dropping shenanigans and would often parade her bevy of beauties around town in a flashy carriage drawn by two trained elk. While most folks seemed to like Laura Bell, the madam still had powerful enemies. The astute businesswoman was constantly fighting legal battles, and it was no secret that city officials wanted her gone. It was rather uncanny when the fat cats at city hall soon got their wish. On January 25, 1918, the evening edition of the *Colorado Springs Gazette* screamed:

GIRL DIES WHEN AUTO TURNS OVER AT CASTLE ROCK
RED LIGHT QUEEN OF COLORADO CITY AND BLIND MAN ARE BADLY HURT

Fifty-seven-year-old Laura Bell McDaniel and her namesake niece, twenty-nine-year-old Little Laura, were taking a blind gentleman to Denver for a doctor's appointment when tragedy struck. Little Laura was driving forty miles per hour when she inexplicably flipped her auntie's new luxury car near the town of Castle Rock. Little Laura was instantly killed when she was thrown from the vehicle, which rolled on top of her. Laura Bell and her friend were rushed to the hospital in Colorado Springs, where she later died. Dusty McCarty was the sole survivor of the tragedy and amazingly walked away with only a broken arm. It was later discovered that the deputy district attorney for Colorado Springs and two of his henchmen were following close behind the doomed trio just before their car went off the road. Laura Bell's camp shouted foul play, but the dead can't talk, and the blind don't make good eyewitnesses. The scandalous rumors were finally put to rest, but only after police records went up in flames—along with the Castle Rock Courthouse!

In 1902, Reverend Duncan Lamont and his wife, Katherine, came all the way from Scotland to civilize the notorious hellhole that Colorado City had become. Mrs. Duncan was soon elected president of the Women's Christian Temperance Union, and her hubby became a highly esteemed member of the school board, postmaster and the minister of the First Baptist Church. The devout couple was accredited with saving quite a few drunkards, gamblers and wayward women but was better known for their rather jubilant ways of preaching the good word. During a January cold snap in 1907, a wicked fire swept down the south side of Colorado Avenue. As hungry flames swallowed the red-light district, the preacher joyfully praised that his prayers had finally been answered. While firemen worked feverishly to extinguish the roaring blaze, the preacher proselytized to the slaves of Devil Rum about his greatest moral victory. Lamont shouted that the wicked city of sin was finally being baptized by fire—just like the biblical towns of Sodom and Gomorrah. Finally, the frenzied firemen grew tired of the ranting reverend and blasted him with the water hose. The shady ladies joined in the fun and baptized the holy man with water buckets! Needless to say, the pillar of society froze into a pillar of ice and had to be carried back to the church to thaw out.

Not long after the wet-and-wild water fight, Colorado City voted to become a dry town, but the mischievous saloonkeepers kept the party going by starting a new wet utopia called Ramona. Ramona was located just a few blocks away from the mother land of Colorado City, rising from the ashes of the red-light district like a phoenix. The exciting enterprise ignited great enthusiasm when it was learned that the new town would be a partier's paradise where anything goes. Over 1,300 rugged individuals signed the petition to incorporate the new oasis, and Colorado soon gave its official stamp of approval. Saloons popped up overnight, and a tent city quickly followed. Ramona elected a mayor and appointed city council members—all of whom just happened to own saloons. During the summer, large tents were set up for Chautauqua-type boxing events, and several championship fights were staged in the manly man's town. By the end of the year, Ramona boasted a population of 300 and had a cigar shop and drugstore but mostly consisted of bawdy establishments. Word about the renegade town worried many, and fear only added fuel to the flames. In the spring of 1914, the *Colorado City Iris* newspaper reached out with headlines that warned:

GRILLS RAMONA IN SERMON ABOUT OUTLAW TOWN
EVANGELIST PRATT TELLS MEN THAT WIDE OPEN TOWNS DO NOT MAKE GOOD BUSINESS

Needless to say, the neighboring dry cities of Colorado Springs and Colorado City were extremely perturbed with Ramona. Colorado Springs was so embarrassed by the scandal that it hastily pulled the plug on the rebel town's water supply. But the ruffians of Ramona just scoffed at the hostile gesture—nobody in their sleazy utopia drank water anyway! The great unwashed of Ramona simply waited for nightfall, tapped Colorado Spring's fire hydrants and secretly filled their water jugs. However, the glorious rebellion was short-lived because the entire state went dry in 1915, and the notorious town of Ramona had no other choice but to pull up its tent stakes.

Both Colorado City and Ramona were later incorporated into Colorado Springs. The notorious town of Ramona was located near present-day Thorndale Park near Twenty-fourth Street and Uintah.

Chapter 16

One-Man Wonders

There is no substitute for hard work. Genius is one percent inspiration and ninety-nine percent perspiration.
—Thomas Edison

Colorado is home to several amazing man-made monuments that confirm the vision, pride, talent and tenacity of the architect. One of these incredible structures is Cano's Castle, which is located in the southern Colorado town of Antonito. Dominic Espinosa, known to locals as Cano, created the towering castle entirely out of recycled items. From a distance, several gleaming beer-can turrets loom over the horizon. Cano began creating his castle over forty years ago and calls this labor of love a work in progress. One can't help but be amazed at the towering hodgepodge marvel, especially considering that the artist works without a net. Another self-made visionary is Jim Bishop, who calls himself a modern-day castle builder. The human dynamo has been featured in both local newspapers and national magazines for almost half a century. Mr. Bishop is an inspiration to many because he built a colossal monument representing personal triumph over naysayers. The self-taught architect/artist dropped out of high school when a teacher told him he would never amount to anything. The ambitious kid saved money from a paper route to buy property in the San Isabel Mountains. Ten years later, he married his sweetheart and built her a rock home using only his bare hands, grit and determination. When his wife told her prince charming that the cottage looked more like a castle, inspiration struck. Without the use of blueprints or power tools, Jim Bishop built a rambling monument for his queen that spirals 160 feet into the heavens. The castle features a grand ballroom, stained glass windows, intricate ironwork and several spiral staircases leading to balconies with bird's-eye views of the forest. Protruding from the metal-and-glass roof is the monstrous head of a fire-breathing dragon, which hovers over the castle like a loyal sentinel. The scrappy Renaissance man promises that Bishop's Castle will always remain free to the public and jokingly calls his masterpiece the poor man's Disneyland. When asked when the castle will be completed, Jim says that his work will be finished the day that he stops breathing. On any summer weekend, you can drop by Bishop's Castle and marvel at the monkey man swinging over sheer rock walls with a bucket of mortar in hand. It's a real

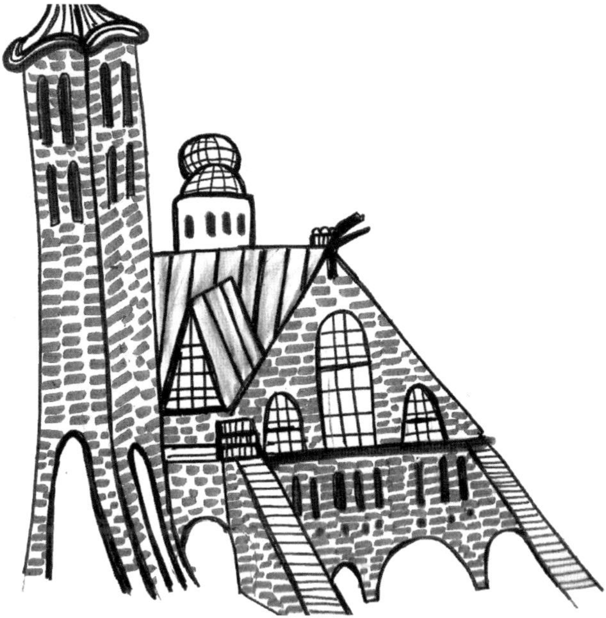

treat watching a living legend at work, and thankfully, it doesn't look like the silver-haired genius will be slowing down anytime soon.

Believe it or not, Cano and Jim Bishop were not the first one-man wonders to build amazing monuments in Colorado. Over one hundred years ago, an impoverished Italian immigrant named Uberto Gibello built a truly amazing underground monument near Julesburg. Now known as the Italian Caves, this underground marvel became a true testament to how far one man can go when he has a good wife behind him.

Uberto Gibello, who would later be known as the "Human Mole," was born in Italy in 1840 and worked as a stonemason and miner until he set sail for the United States in 1880. He worked for the Union Pacific Railroad until he saved enough money to start a homestead near Julesburg in 1887. Homesick for good Italian wine, Uberto planted a vineyard, which he irrigated by digging cement-lined trenches from the South Platte River. But despite the sophisticated system, the grapes withered on the vine, and he lost his life's savings on the disastrous enterprise. Sadly, Uberto was forced to give up farming on his infertile land and became a water witch, finding and digging wells for local farmers. Legend holds that Uberto learned the trick of dowsing, or water witching, in his homeland of Italy, where his grandfather taught him to make dowsing rods from tree branches. Uberto became well known around Julesburg for his unique talent and for being a tad peculiar (he lived in a tent like a hermit on his barren land). But most folks in Julesburg liked Uberto despite his quirky reputation. Why did the Human Mole begin his obsessive digging? Perhaps the Italian was inspired by a unique sod home built nearby by German bachelor Charles Leeks. Leeks fashioned the underground shelter in the shape of a stone jug and used the long, narrow neck leading to the surface as a periscope. Subterranean structures were popular during pioneer times, mostly because they provided ideal protection from Indian raids.

And so it was that the Human Mole labored by the sweat of his brow and excavated his worthless, barren property until a modest sod home was finished. Thrilled with his success, the Italian dynamo dug another underground sanctuary that was bigger and better than the first. Then, for the next twenty-three years, the dynamic digger continued tunneling into the earth by dim lantern light; using only a pickaxe, a shovel and a sturdy wheelbarrow he jokingly called his "wife." The lifelong bachelor dug a complicated series of underground rooms connected by a 9-foot-wide tunnel that stretched over half a mile. The largest cavern was over 350 feet in length, 6 feet tall and 10 feet wide. A stone staircase led down to a 150-foot foyer in which pictures were hung on the dirt walls. Some of the rooms had furniture carved from dirt and featured sod beds, tables and niches carved into the walls. A few of the rooms featured 60-foot-deep water wells that were powered by aboveground windmills. Uberto guarded his incredible underground den with the fierce pride of a lion. In fact, when historians tried to restore the old Platte Trail, which ran through his property, he flatly denied them access and even dug a deep trench across his road to prohibit trespassing. Some reports stated that the old man demanded that travelers paid a fee when passing through his land and shot at those who did not comply. As time went on, the people of Julesburg thought Uberto was going mad as they watched the recluse haul rock hither and yon, day after day. When asked by a bystander why he worked so hard, Uberto simply replied that he had to work hard because he didn't want to get sick and die. But mental illness finally claimed the life of the robust seventy-five-year-old hermit. On Friday, September 10, 1910, the *Denver Post* reported that the Italian immigrant had bit the dust, with headlines shouting:

TWO EAT BAKED SAND; ONE DIES, OTHER KEEPS ON
DENVER CARPENTER THINKS DIET IS CURING HIM OF DISPEPSIA
HERMIT IS DEAD
JULESBURG RECLUSE NOT SO SUCCESFUL WITH SAME REMEDY

The article reported that Denver carpenter C.J. Hendershott had been eating sand to cure his indigestion and that Uberto Gibello died at his homestead a few days earlier, a victim of the same bogus folk remedy. Apparently, the old recluse was eating baked sand three times a day in order to cure an obstinate case of indigestion. Uberto's stiff corpse was found in his underground dirt palace lying peacefully on his lumpy sod bed. The old man was wearing his best bib and tucker, his red skull cap smashed typically over a mop of cotton-white hair. Sitting next to the bed was the faithful wheelbarrow he called wife, filled with rocks and sand. Oddly, the old Italian died with a clump of soil stuck in his mouth, and a half-eaten pan of baked dirt lay nearby. No one in town seemed to know how long the poor old man had been baking and ingesting dirt, but everyone agreed that the recluse had not been seen at the supermarket for quite awhile. A local chapter of nuns paid for the old miser's funeral.

Despite the old man's obvious poverty, rumors swirled that he had gold dust secretly buried in his underground palace. Treasure hunters came from all over the area in search of riches but were disappointed when nothing was found. Years later, the hermit's underground palace became an unofficial tourist attraction known as the Italian Caves, and curiosity seekers came from all over the region to investigate the former home of the Human Mole. Now all that is left of Uberto Gibello's underground empire are the crumbled remains of a few caved-in tunnels and a historical marker near the highway. However, because of his sheer determination and gumption, the Human Mole of Colorado will be forever known, just like living legends Cano and his castle-building contemporary Jim Bishop.

Cano's Castle is located on the main drag as you drive south into Antonito. Bishop's Castle is located on Highway 165 near Rye and is open from dawn to dusk during the summer. Just look for the castle mailbox on Highway 165 or call 719-485-3040.

Uberto Gibello is buried in the Julesburg Cemetery, and the historical marker for the Italian Caves can be seen just outside town.

Chapter 17

Serpent Slayers

In revenge and in love, woman is more barbarous than man.
—Friedrich Nietzsche

No one can argue that women were tough as nails back in the olden days, and a few in Colorado became notorious for their true grit. One amazing story centers on a diminutive young woman named Mrs. Slaughterback, who singlehandedly slaughtered dozens of diamondback rattlesnakes near Platteville. The amazing feat won the young divorcée the honorable reputation as a sharpshooter and the nickname "Rattlesnake Kate." The legend of Rattlesnake Kate began when she and her young son went duck hunting on October 28, 1925. Kate nearly had a hissy fit when a huge hungry-looking rattler suddenly slithered onto their path, but the quick-thinking mother blew the reptile's head off with one blast from her Winchester just seconds before it was about to strike her young son. Happy with her kill, Kate threw the plump prize into her satchel, planning to serve it for supper, and then confidently continued strolling toward the pond.

Just moments later, several more angry snakes seeking revenge slithered toward her, but the young mother aimed calmly and fired at every vile serpent that crossed her path until she ran out of bullets. Kate nearly panicked when the snakes kept coming at them from every direction, but the desperate divorcée ripped a No Hunting sign off a fence post and used the business end to club the vindictive vipers. Two horrendous hours later, the rattled woman stood triumphantly over 140 slaughtered serpents, which she later tanned and fashioned into a lovely dress, matching headband, necklace and shoes. News of the seemingly superhuman seamstress spread like wildfire, and the young divorcee was often asked to sport the handmade rattlesnake dress at social functions.

The feisty woman enjoyed basking in the limelight for the rest of her life and had several newspaper articles written about her exploits. During the middle of World War II, the *San Diego Union* newspaper ran an article on March 29, 1942,

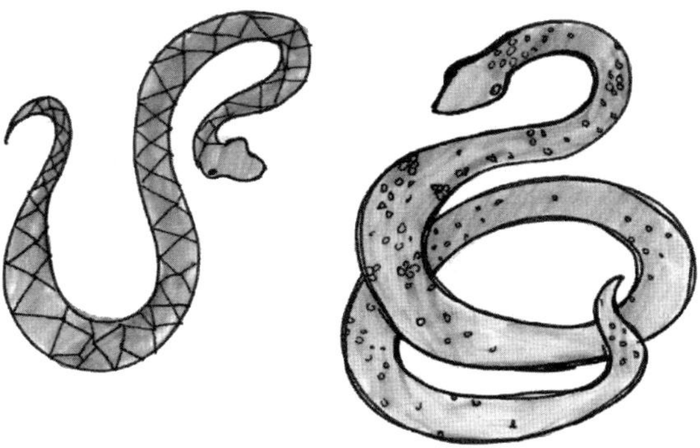

suggesting that brave Rattlesnake Kate join the battlefront. The headlines blared, "WOMAN SNAKE FIGHTER READY IF JAPS COME." The article went on to say that the Colorado pioneer woman was ready for battle and how the sharpshooter was a veritable Annie Oakley with her gun. Rattlesnake Kate capitalized on her fame by starting a snake farm, where she harvested venom, skins and rattles and preserved them using her homespun taxidermy skills. Kate Slaughterback was an old woman when she died in 1969. The spunky seamstress was proud to have never lived down her hard-won nickname—perhaps that is why "Rattlesnake Kate" was engraved on her tombstone in Mizpah Cemetery near Greely, Colorado.

Thereby hangs the tale of Mountain Charley, another feisty character who became infamous for revenge and made quite an impression on the founding father of Greely, Colorado. Horace Greely was credited with urging Americans to "Go West, young man" and was reportedly pleased as punch to finally meet the infamous oddball at Gregory Diggings back in 1859. When Horace first came face to face with the living legend, he noticed that the young lad was suspiciously missing an Adam's apple and whiskers; then it dawned on him that he was really a she. The diminutive, cross-dressing mountain mama had quite a reputation in the territory as an accomplished gunslinger. Mountain Charley was described as an attractive woman who preferred to dress like a man but never bothered to hide her ample charms. Like many of the other men living in the gold camp, Charley was running from her past and had a story to hide. Mountain Charley began life as Elsa Jane Forest and became a child bride at fourteen. A few years later, her husband, a respected gentleman gambler, was ruthlessly murdered on a Mississippi River boat. Mr. Jamieson was tried for the murder, yet the lowdown snake was never convicted for the crime. Without her husband's income, the young widow was forced to sell everything she owned, including her long, beautiful honey-brown hair. Elsa used most of the money to put her two young daughters in the benevolent care of the Sisters of Mercy. The young woman reluctantly traded her frilly dresses, dainty slippers and lacey shawls for men's attire and worked as a cabin boy, planning to hunt down the riverboat thief who murdered her husband and then shoot him dead. Five long years later, Charley ran into Jamieson at a gambling dive in Saint Louis. That night, Charley triumphantly announced her true identity and revengeful intent to send him to hell in a handbasket! Guns were fired; a bullet sliced through Jamieson's arm, and another ripped into Charley's leg. When the gunslingers ran out of bullets, they sheepishly limped away, swearing to one day settle the score once and for all.

When Charley learned that Jamieson had escaped to Colorado and become a prospector, she worked for the railroad until she had earned enough money to follow him there. In the gold camp of Gregory Diggings, she cast her bread upon the water and opened a bakery. By and by, the mountain mama saved enough money to later start up a watering hole in Denver. By that time, everyone was calling her Mountain Charley, and so accordingly she named her new digs the Mountain Boy Saloon. The bawdy establishment attracted the rowdiest of ruffians and was just the kind of place that a lowlife snake like Jamieson would likely slither into one day. Business thrived at Mountain Charley's infamous saloon, yet she still did not have peace in her heart. Charley dreamed night and day about brutally torturing her archenemy, and the dark obsession haunted her very soul.

Finally, in the spring of 1860, Mountain Charley had her golden day in the sun—ironically just outside the mining camp of Golden. She was heading to the town on business when she spied a man who looked similar to Jamieson riding a mule toward her. The bright afternoon sun blinded Charley's eyes, and she could not distinguish her hated rival for certain. Apparently, the coward didn't have the common courtesy to properly introduce himself before firing his rifle directly at her. Seconds later, a screaming bullet whizzed by Charley's head, quickly gaining her attention. Despite her disadvantage, Mountain Charley fired blindly into the glaring sun, and in a blaze of glory, her nemesis fell from his mount. Not satisfied with the victory, Charley gleefully unloaded her pistol several times and then jumped from her horse when she ran out of bullets. After noticing that her adversary was still kicking, Charley pulled a knife from her boot and was about to jab Jamieson in the jugular when fate intervened. Three men rode up just in the knick of time and demanded an explanation from the trigger- and dagger-happy cross-dressing cowboy. Charley desperately pleaded her case, but the men said further action would be for the law to decide and then loaded the pitiful victim into their wagon. Charley begrudgingly went along for the ride but began having a grand old time after watching her victim's horrific struggle. Every time the cart hit a rock or swerved to avoid a pothole, Jamieson cried out in excruciating agony, and Charley roared with gut-wrenching laughter. The vile vixen shamelessly taunted her enemy, adding insult to his injuries by spitting tobacco in his bullet wounds and whistling "Dixie" along the way. By the time they reached the doctor's office, Charley was mighty thirsty and wanted to celebrate.

The cross-dresser threw one hell of a shindig that night and was surprised to fall head over heels for a much younger man. The handsome cowboy was apparently attracted to vindictive women who looked like men, and so the unlikely duo was a match made in heaven. Mountain Charley was eventually cleared of murder charges because Jamieson remarkably survived. However, the Grim Reaper eventually caught up with the snake four years later, and when Mountain Charley heard that the yellow-bellied coward had died from yellow fever, she couldn't help but laugh at the poetic justice. Thankfully, true love had already set her heart free from the horrendous hatred that plagued her for so long.

Years later, Mountain Charley wrote an autobiography about her infamous life. The cross-dressing mountain mama will always be remembered in Colorado for her dogged determination to hunt down the snake who murdered her first husband, and so her brazen spirit lives on in legends of the Old West—just like Rattlesnake Kate.

To see the snakeskin dress and other fashionable serpent accessories created by Rattlesnake Kate, please visit the Greely History Museum.

Kate Slaughterback's actual farmhouse can now be seen at the Centennial Village Museum in Greely. Call 970-350-9220.

Chapter 18

Jinxed Gemstones

Oh what a tangled web we weave, when first we practice to deceive!
—Walter Scott

The Hope Diamond is better known for its infamous deadly curse than its priceless beauty. Supposedly, over one hundred owners from monarchs to aristocrats either suffered or died under the gemstone's deadly spell. Thankfully, the Hope Diamond is now housed under lock and key in the Smithsonian, where it can do no more harm. Interestingly enough, there are a few other legendary gems associated with a deadly jinx, and both were owned by Colorado con men who perished because of their so-called hoodoo. One of these curious gemstones is the Pearl of Lao Tzu, better known as the Pearl of Allah. This whopping fourteen-pounder is known as the largest pearl in the world, according to both Ripley's and Guinness. Practically speaking, the gaudy grey pearl could never be fashioned into jewelry and might be better suited as a bowling ball. Obviously valued for its rare colossal size, the odd-looking artifact closely resembles the size and shape of a human brain, which might partially explain the strange legends associated with it. The most popular story tells that the hideous pearl was cultivated by Chinese philosopher/spiritualist Lao-Tzu, who placed a sacred jade amulet in a clamshell over 2,500 years ago. Over the centuries, various custodians transferred the incubated pearl into bigger clamshells as it evolved. During this time, several wars erupted over guardianship of the sacred clam, convincing Chinese monks of its ancient curse. Fearing for their lives, a priest finally shipped the colossal clam to a secret location for safekeeping. Tragically, the Chinese ship sank during a storm, and the holy mollusk was lost to the depths of the Palawan Sea. Centuries later, a diver in the Philippines was astonished when he came across the unusually large clamshell. Once the young native pried the massive mollusk open, he was mysteriously struck dead by a bolt of lightning. Natives understandably feared the awesome power of the wicked gem. Eventually, the tribal chieftain gave the ugly pearl to a doctor for saving his son's life, telling him that he must keep the gem for twenty-one years or he, too, would suffer the pearl's evil wrath. However, the doctor sold the ancient treasure just as soon as he reached the California coastline. Ironically, his infant son died the very next day. Colorado Springs resident and alleged gangster Joseph Bonicelli bought a third interest in the Pearl of Allah back in 1990, when it was valued at a cool one hundred million clams. Shortly thereafter, his wife was found murdered, and the gangster was implicated in the crime and sentenced to life in prison. Mr. Bonicelli suddenly died in 1996, and the mysterious Pearl of Allah is now the property of

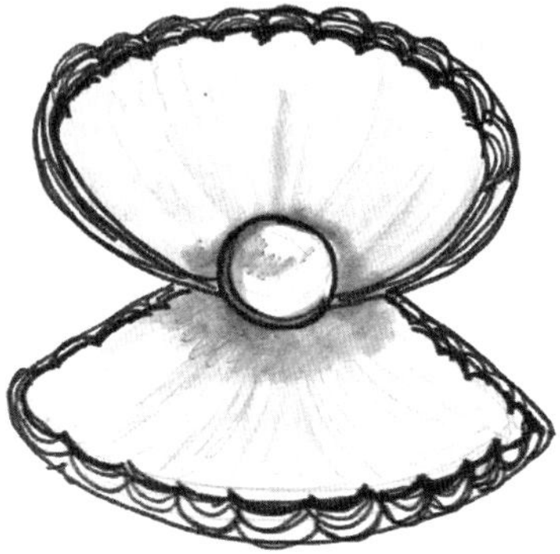

a probate court, which is probably the safest place for the jinxed gemstone.

The Kelly Diamond was also well known for its fabled deadly curse, but what makes this story so interesting is not how the gem was created but the way in which it was consumed—both literally and figuratively. The story begins with an affable character by the name of Singapore Jake who traveled all over the country benefitting folks with his carpetbag of herbal remedies, charms and talismans. In 1880, the traveling snake-oil salesman decided to settle down, hanging his shingle in Denver. Old Jake couldn't read or write much, but he could skillfully interpret tea leaves, crystal balls and tarot cards and was considered a wise prophet by many who knew him. Early pioneers, ranchers, farmers and even the blue bloods of Capitol Hill went all the way to the shady Chinatown district just to pay the old prophet a visit. Prospectors and gamblers were especially interested in seeking his sage advice, especially when their good luck soured. Folks told of how Singapore Jake could go into a pretty good trance for just one dollar, but for five bucks, he would make his eyes bulge in a weirdly penetrative way and his body shake with powerful might. Supposedly, the mysterious prophet studied the occult in India, but it was later revealed that the only Indians he ever really saw in his lifetime were the local Sioux, Cheyenne and Arapahoe.

Singapore Jake enjoyed the sweet taste of success for many good years until his career came to a screeching halt. Jake's bad luck began when he came into direct contact with the infamous Kelly Diamond. The brilliant three-carrot bobble was fashioned into a beautiful stickpin by its original owner, who died the first time he wore it, igniting rumors about the jinxed gemstone. The diamond was later named after a gentleman gunslinger known as King Kelly. Kelly won the diamond stickpin in a poker game but was shot down in cold blood before leaving the card table. After the gunslinger's death, the diamond was given to his lover, a soiled dove. The next day, she, too, was found murdered while wearing the jinxed gem. Detectives never found a motive or suspects in either case, and both crimes remain unsolved. The gunslinger's lover racked up a considerable lodging bill at the time of her untimely death, and so the diamond was given to hotel owner Marty McGraw as generous compensation. McGraw laughed off rumors about the deadly stickpin's so-called hoodoo and proudly sported the ill-gotten Kelly diamond wherever he went. Sadly, just a week later, McGraw's wife ran off with a man from Frisco, and he was robbed of several thousand dollars. McGraw's pals beseeched him to seek help from Singapore Jake before it was too late. Although the hotel owner was skeptical of the old soothsayer's charms, he must have figured he had nothing else left to lose.

Singapore Jake was confident about being able to remove the deadly curse from the diamond but grimly stated that the procedure would be costly. After Marty agreed on the price, the mystic popped the diamond in his mouth to suck it dry of the hoodoo and then slipped behind a curtain to procure the necessary tools needed to complete the exorcism. The mysterious antechamber held various clay bowls filled with herbal remedies, assorted magical implements and a tall glass jar filled with rhinestones of various sizes. (The fake diamonds were switched with real ones whenever the opportunity presented itself.) Just when the good-for-nothing soothsayer was about to pull a fast one, a wild-eyed man accused of being a cheat came running into the fortuneteller's den seeking refuge. When Jake heard the commotion, he bolted from behind the curtain and was plowed over by the panicked gambler, causing him to accidently swallow the jinxed Kelly diamond. Mr. McGraw grabbed the soothsayer by his bootstraps, turning him upside down in hopes of extracting the costly gem from the old man's gullet while the desperate gambler hollered for a doctor. Luckily, a young dentist who had always been curious to see the insides of a living man just happened to be strolling by, and he gleefully volunteered to perform the impromptu surgery. However, Singapore Jake was not about to be operated on—especially not by a rookie dentist! Thinking quickly, Jake grabbed his bag of tricks, hopped on his pony and rode like a bat out of hell toward the mountains. Moments later, the crafty snake-oil salesman was surprised as hell when he saw Marty McGraw, the cheating gambler and the anxious dentist following in hot pursuit. After several hours, the exhausted soothsayer reached a ridge overlooking a placid mountain lake and turned to survey his situation. The soothsayer soon realized that he was caught between the devil and the deep blue sea when he spied the persistent trio not far behind. Then, in the twinkling of an eye, the loose gravel gave way, and Singapore Jake fell head over heels into the lake below. Mr. McGraw and the gambler fainted after watching the con man topple over the cliff, and the rookie dentist was obviously perturbed as well. Years later, the *Denver Post* recapped the strange escapade in an article headlined:

HOODOO OF KELLY DIAMOND
END OF SINGPORE JAKE
EARLY DAY MYSTIC FAILS IN A PLOT TO PINCH BIG ROCK AND ENDS IN WATERY GRAVE

Whatever became of the cheating gambler and rookie dentist no one can say, but Marty McGraw lived to be a wealthy old man, and he finally conceded that the tragic ending of the jinxed Kelly diamond really did have a happy ending after all.

The History Colorado Center is a fabulous new museum in Denver at the corner of Twelfth and Broadway. For more information, call 303-449-8679.

Chapter 19

Manly Man-eaters

They say that bread is the staff of life, but I say it's fresh meat.
—Chef Boyardee

Wild game dishes like smoked antelope, buffalo and venison, as well as Rocky Mountain oysters, have always been popular with locals. The Native Americans and early pioneers were the first to enjoy roasting wild game in the great outdoors, but Colorado mountain man Alfred Packer was the first to become famous for his avant-garde campfire recipes. Packer even had a restaurant named after him posthumously and was the inspiration for several cookbooks, kitchen calendars and even a musical. Packer's rise to culinary fame began on November 17, 1873, when he joined a group of twenty-one prospectors from Utah who were heading to Colorado seeking riches. By the time the caravan reached the halfway point near the present-day town of Delta, they were already a month behind schedule. Ute Indian chief Ouray wisely advised the prospectors to wait until springtime to cross the treacherous snow-capped mountains, but a few of them with ants in their pants decided to go on ahead to Breckenridge. The prospectors agreed to continue the risky journey under the expert guidance of Alfred Packer. Sixty-five days later, Alfred Packer wandered into the Los Pinos Indian Agency, looking like death warmed over. The wild-eyed mountain man offered several excuses for the absence of his prospecting partners, eventually telling officials that he was an epileptic and that his illness had frightened his friends, who ran off and left him high and dry in the howling wilderness to survive on nothing but wishes.

After just a few days' rest, Packer headed to the nearest saloon to celebrate life anew. In the nearby settlement of Saguache, the mountain man had a grand old time flaunting his shiny new Winchester rifle, handsome buck knife and oodles of cash. Some folks around town were familiar with Packer's reputation as a broken-down drunkard and grew suspicious. On a hunch, the local sheriff arrested the mountain man and held him at the Saguache jail until authorities could arrive for further questioning. Meanwhile, a posse was sent out to search for the five missing miners. A few days later, journalists for *Harpers Weekly* were on assignment near Lake City and decided to take a buggy ride outside Gunnison. When they came across the South Fork River, the journalists stopped for a picnic. However, an artist named John Randolph nearly lost his lunch when he stumbled across a gruesome discovery—five dead prospectors were found huddled together under a sweeping pine tree. At first, Randolph figured that the men had frozen to death, but upon closer examination, he observed bullet holes and realized that the victims had been murdered. One of the men, his head bashed in, lay a few feet from the others, and another was missing his skull. Oddly, all of the corpses had big hunks of flesh sliced from their bones. Randolph quickly realized that he'd accidently stumbled across an abandoned cannibal camp. The artist busily sketched the horrendous murder scene in grim, graphic detail. Within days, news of a man-eater at large quickly spread across the country—much to the embarrassment of Colorado tourism agents. As soon as Alfred learned that federal authorities were coming to investigate the murders, he made a daring jail break. Headlines in the September 11, 1874 *New York Herald* reported:

A WHITE CANNIBAL
HORRIBLE DEED IN THE WILDS OF THE ROCKY MOUNTAINS
A MINER KILLS AND EATS FIVE OF HIS COMPANIONS
A SICKENING DIET
DISCOVERY OF THE MUTILATED CORPSES…
THE MURDERER IS STILL AT LARGE

The wild man was on the lam for nine long years until he was inadvertently spotted by a former colleague at Fort Fetterman, Wyoming. Frenchy Cabazon, one of the original twenty-one prospectors, recognized Packer immediately when he saw his missing finger and heard his girlish voice. Days later, the nine-fingered, sissy-voiced cannibal was extradited back to Lake City. After a spectacular trial, Alfred was pronounced guilty of premeditated murder on April 13, 1883, and sentenced to hang a month later. According to Christopher O'Brien's intriguing book *Enter the Valley*, district court judge Melville B. Gerry handed down the sentence by addressing Alfred Packer with the following statement:

> *Packer, ye man-eating son-of-a-bitch, there was just seven Democrats in Hinsdale County, and ye ate five of them, damn ye! I sentence you to be hanged by the neck until dead, dead, dead. Whether your murderous hand was guided by the misty light of the moon, of the flickering blaze of a campfire, only you can tell. No eye saw the bloody deed performed. No ear save your own caught the dying cries of your victims. To the sickening details of your crime I will not refer. Silence is kindness. I do not say things to harrow your soul, for I know you have drunk from the cup of bitterness to its very dregs.*

In another twist of fate, a stay of execution was granted because Packer claimed his trial was unconstitutional.

While the courts battled over what was to become of the prisoner, the cannibal became a national curiosity. The "Colorado Cannibal" delighted in crafting watch chains, necklaces and bracelets braided from his long black hair and made a good living selling such novelties to tourists. He was tried again and was again found guilty; however, Governor Thomas granted him parole in 1901. Six years later, Alfred Packer died while awaiting a governmental pardon. Headlines in the April 29, 1907 issue of the *Trenton Evening Times* reported:

COLORADO'S "MAN EATER" IS DEAD
ALFERD PACKER OF CANNIBILISTIC FAME
DIES ON LONE RANCH IN FACE OF PARDON

Ironically, the sixty-five-year-old cannibal died of stomach problems, and when it was reported in the newspaper, many thought it was just a tongue-in-cheek joke. After his death, journalists wrote of a misunderstood mountain man but noted that at least his name was spelled correctly on his Littleton tombstone. Alfred had his name tattooed on his arm, but the dyslexic artist mistakenly spelled it "Alferd," which caused a lifetime of confusion. The celebrated cannibal might be humored to know that a café in Boulder was named (although also misspelled) in his honor. In 1968, the Alferd G. Packer Memorial Grill opened its doors on the University of Colorado campus with the slogan "Have a friend for lunch."

Charles Gardner loved his friends to death, but the mountain man might have had a bone to pick with fellow cannibal Alfred Packer. Both men were from Pennsylvania and migrated to Colorado around the same time, yet Alfred was a much more celebrated cannibal than Charles ever was. After learning about Charlie's volcanic appetite, it might make you wonder why he is not the better known of the hated man-eaters. As Charles Gardner grew up, his teachers said he was as dull as bathwater and his folks complained that the big galoot ate them out of house and home. When the overgrown teenager turned sixteen, he became known as the devil incarnate after killing his first man—who just so happened to be a Catholic priest. In Leavenworth City, the goliath became known as Big Phil and hooked up with a couple of army deserters who went by the names of Alson and Merrick. The troublemakers soon learned of an oldster who was hoarding a small fortune and decided to steal it. Late one night, the trio crept into the old man's house and robbed him of his savings. The next morning, neighbors found the poor old man tied to his bedpost, dead from fright. Outraged citizens formed a posse to hunt down the brazen robbers, and bloodhounds led them to a deserted barn. The posse hogtied Alson and Merrick and tortured them for hours without mercy. Finally, the thieves were thrown onto a raging bonfire, and the vigilantes laughed until their victims' screams faded into the night. Big Phil, who was hiding in a haystack, was mighty aroused by the savory aroma of fresh meat roasting over the coals, so when the coast was clear, he crept over to grab a bite. Gardner was horrified when he recognized the smoldering remains of his companions but politely toasted to their memory before devouring the hula girl tattooed on Merrick's forearm. It was the first time that Big Phil would ever eat the flesh of his friends, but tragically, it would not be the last.

It wasn't until 1884 that Gardner was officially labeled a man-eater. That winter, Big Phil and an Indian scout were sent from Fort Laramie to go on a mountain mission, but when a brutal blizzard hit the Rockies, everyone assumed that they both had died. Several weeks later, the soldiers were shocked when the mountain man came stumbling back into camp. Big Phil claimed that he had to eat his mule just to survive the bitter storm. When the soldiers asked what happened to his Indian guide, the cannibal chuckled before throwing down the withered black stump of a human leg. Big Phil boasted that it was all that was left of his juicy, young Indian friend. Needless to say, the mountain man was feared all over the western frontier, and stories about his culinary escapades grew wilder as the years went by. Soldier Charlie Jones was camped with Kit Carson near Denver's Cherry Creek when Gardner filled his belly with an exotic dish that he called Klock Stew. Jones grew suspicious when he realized that Klock was the name of Big Phil's devoted Indian wife. The sergeant joked that Big Phil was the only man who didn't have to leave his tepee to hunt for supper. On January 3, 1887, the *Rocky Mountain*

News featured a story about the mountain man's adventures with a blunt article and the following headlines:

CANNIBAL PHIL
PHILADELPHIA OUTLAW TURNS
CANNIBAL ON THE PACIFIC COAST
HUMAN FIEND TOASTING AND
DEVOURING THE FLESH OF HIS
COMPANIONS

When an editor for the *Rocky Mountain News* asked what human flesh tasted like, Big Phil told him that any flesh tasted good when cooked but that the hands, feet and head of a human being were delicious even when eaten raw. When asked what meat human flesh could be compared to, Big Phil bluntly stated that the texture was a lot like pigskin but that it tasted just like chicken. Gardner was never arrested for the atrocities committed against his companions, perhaps because most of them were Indians. No one really knows whatever became of Big Phil, but it is generally believed that the mountain man was killed in a barroom brawl in Montana during the winter of 1874—which was incidentally the same year that his kindred brother, Alferd Packer, took a hankering to human flesh. Maybe the former Pennsylvanians were just missing a great Philly cheesesteak.

The Hinsdale County Museum in Lake City offers haunted history tours during the summer. For more information, please call 970-944-2515.

If you would like to sit in the actual prison cell in which Alfred Packer did time in the state penitentiary, visit the enthralling Museum of Colorado Prisons at 201 North First Street in Canon City. This museum is rumored to be haunted. www.prisonmuseum.org.

Chapter 20

Cons and Creeps

It's no wonder that truth is stranger than fiction; fiction has to make sense.
—Mark Twain

D.C. Oakes was a pioneer and prospector who co-wrote an infamous guidebook with an impressive name: *Discoveries of the South Platte River by Luke Tierney to Which Is Appended a Guide to the Route by Smith and Oakes*. The book greatly exaggerated the ease of striking it rich in Colorado and ignited gold rush fever. In 1859, an estimated 150,000 easterners migrated to the Colorado Territory during the ensuing Pikes Peak or Bust gold rush in hope of striking it rich. Meanwhile, Oakes set up a lumberyard in anticipation of coming business and made himself a rich man. Hundreds of disappointed miners returned to the East Coast, disillusioned by the golden promises by what became known as the Oakes

Hoax, and the swindler was burned in effigy around many campfires.

Practical jokes were all the rage in the late 1800s. Miners in Central City salted a mine to fool prospector Horace Greely into thinking that it was loaded with gold. The hoax not only got a good laugh but also inspired pranksters around the Centennial State to try and top their shenanigans. One of the biggest pranksters of all was a short-statured easterner named Orth Stein, who became an infamous writer for the *Leadville Chronicle*. When Mr. Stein arrived in Leadville in 1880, there were eighty-two saloons, twenty-one gambling halls, thirty-five bordellos, thirty-eight restaurants and three newspapers. Orth knew that if he was going to be a successful reporter, he would have to be competitive, so he did what any creative-minded genius would do—he began "stretching the blanket." Newspapers flew off the shelves. Mr. Stein, being too clever by half, was promoted to top dog. As the money rolled in, the crap got deeper. The only problem was that many people took Orth's solemn word for God's holy truth! Sometimes the little man's tall tales caused big problems, like when crowds lined around the Clarendon block to see an archeological relic that Orth dug out of a cave—the petrified shoe of a caveman. The sheriff had to pull double duty just to establish crowd control, but the fabled stone shoe and Orth Stein were no-shows. It seemed like Stein was always finding archaic relics in caves, and once he even found a sailboat! Stein is also believed to be behind a long-running joke about a mysterious cave near Buena Vista. The story went that the cavern was originally discovered by pioneers heading to California. When the party entered the mouth of the cavern, they were immediately frightened by a strange buzzing sound and discovered thousands of sparrow-sized, long-legged spiders spinning intricate webs of fine silk. The elusive arachnids were angered by the intrusion and devoured the pioneers, and all that remained was a hastily penned warning to others. The hapless Argonauts were just the first of many to be eaten alive in the deadly spider cave. Eventually, a few brave folks captured the industrious spiders and then used their fine silk and tanned hides to make fine-quality gloves. It was later discovered that the long-legged spiders made useful pets. In fact, the daughter of a Salida rancher claimed that her pet spider was a wonderful companion and even slept on her bedpost at night. She quipped that her Prince Charming ate anything you gave him and especially liked cake, candy and ice cream. News of the miraculous spider cave spread across the country. The infamous hoax played out for years until the joke was finally revealed in a 1911 issue of the *Denver Post*, which announced:

FINE GLOVES MADE FROM SPIDER SKINS
IN COLORADO
FAKE? YES, JUST ONE OF THE MANY
SELLS OF WORLD-WIDE FAME
SOME NOTEABLE YARNS
STATE BROADLY ADVERTISED BY SOME
INGENIOUS AND IMPOSSIBLE TALES

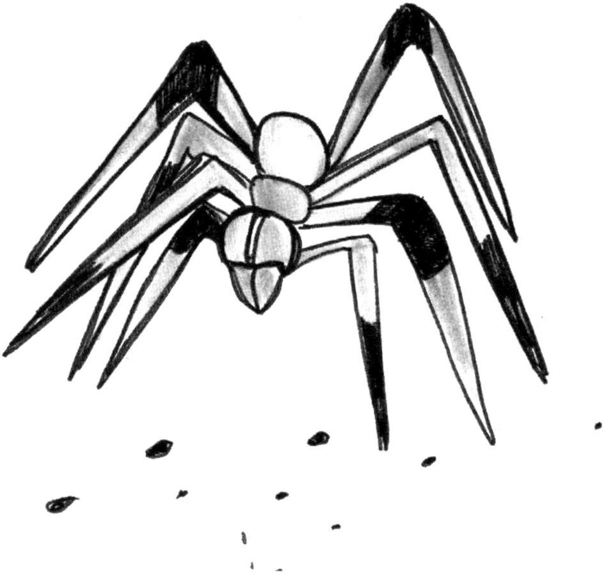

Another infamous prank was pulled in 1878, when a wrestler by the name of William Muldoon was digging out a cave near Beulah and discovered the stone body of a gigantic prehistoric man. The fascinating relic weighed in at 450 pounds and was nearly seven feet tall. The strange fossil became known as the Solid Muldoon and was exhibited throughout the country. Infamous circus promoter P.T. Barnum helped promote the attraction, and the fossil was also owned by infamous Colorado con man Soapy Smith for a time. Soapy exhibited the curiosity in Creed, where it was advertised as the "Petrified Man." Soapy displayed the enigma in dimly lit backrooms of saloons and funeral parlors, where folks paid anywhere from a nickel to a buck each just to get a peep or brief touch of the stone-cold giant. Soapy memorized quite a few fancy facts to impress folks with his knowledge about the prehistoric wonder and consequently made an embarrassment of riches. When the novelty eventually wore off, the stone man was sold to a circus. After traveling around for several years, the weary stone man finally crumbled to dust. The Solid Muldoon ended up being made from cement but sure made its owners a lot of coin. The stone giant was later memorialized with a wooden grave marker that still stands over his pretend grave near Beulah.

Despite these amusing stories, a very real menace threatened the livelihood and sanity of Coloradoans for several decades. The chaos began in the summer of 1890 when folks in the agricultural hamlet of Yuma trembled in silence as they watched the cloudless sky suddenly turn black as night. At first, folks wondered if they were experiencing a solar eclipse, but then they heard a dull hiss rumbling over the horizon. Within minutes, millions of hungry locusts were raiding picnic baskets and jumping into clothing and upswept hairdos. The beady-eyed grasshoppers nibbled on everything in sight and were unlike any grass-chomping creature the town had ever seen. They were twice the size of the common prairie grasshopper, and their long, sticky legs could propel them nearly ten feet in any direction. Most unsettling of all was the bubbling black goo that they spit all over everything and the loud hissing noise they made night

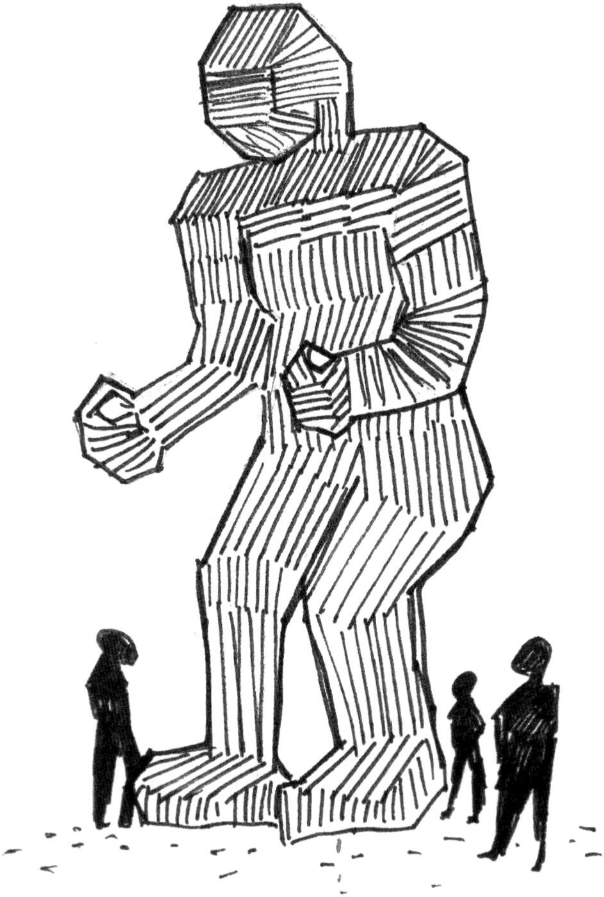

and day. In 1910, the *Gazette Telegraph* reported that locusts were affecting not only local crops but also transportation. The paper's July 19 headlines blared, "TRAINS IMPEDED BY GRASSHOPPER SCOURGE."

It's hard to believe, but trains in Denver's Grand Central Station were actually paralyzed because of the menacing creatures. For decades, farmers scoured almanacs looking for tricks to solve the problem, but to no avail. Needless to say, Coloradoans were panicked. Headlines in the *Colorado Springs Gazette* looked hopeful when it was announced, "MILLIONS OF CORPSES STREW EAST COLORADO BATTLEFIELD."

Eventually, chemical weapons were used against the pests, but results were mixed. Finally, Coloradoans decided to embrace their problem rather than trying to fix it. Folks began scooping the pesky critters up and baking them into pies, cakes and cookies. As one old woman joked, "When life gives you lemons, you make lemonade—and when it gives you grasshoppers, make grasshopper pie!" Folks also began using the grasshoppers in crafts. One lady pressed the creepy critters into photo frames, much like you would do with butterfly wings or flower petals. Another ingenious woman fashioned the pesky insects into bracelets, belts and earrings and then sold the trinkets at the train stop. Folks in Colorado Springs decided to make light of the situation by hosting the annual Soap Weed and Grasshopper Days, a three-day allergy festival dedicated to the love of all things that make your eyes water and skin itch. By the following summer, Coloradoans were actually looking forward to the grasshoppers' arrival and compared the excitement to the return of the swallows to San Juan Capistrano. Sadly, the grasshoppers were no-shows. It was as if the creatures knew they were being exploited by Coloradoans, and so they moved on to Texas, where I hear the grasshoppers have grown as large as pick-up trucks.

For more information about local lore, please visit the Colorado Springs Pioneer Museum at 215 South Tejon Street or call 719-385-5990.

Chapter 21

Vampires and Witches

There is nothing impossible in the existence of the supernatural; its existence seems to me decidedly probable.
—George Santayana

Legends of bloodsucking vampires lurking about in Colorado have been whispered about ever since eastern European miners immigrated to the state and spread frightening stories about the supernatural beings. In 1906, a delusional tramp murdered a well-known Las Animas farmer to drink his warm blood, leading many to accuse him of vampirism. Even today, people believe a popular legend about a so-called vampire's grave in the quaint village of La Fayette. The long-forgotten grave actually belongs to two European immigrants who died during the Spanish flu epidemic in 1918. Cemetery records reveal that the men didn't know each other and that they died on different days but were interred in the same plot, a common practice when burying the indigent. The spooky rumors began long ago, when on full-moon nights, a mysterious cloaked figure was seen lurking about in Pauper's Field. Most folks dismissed the man as a lunatic, but when a tall, straggly tree grew out of the plot where the stranger was seen, cemetery officials took notice. Maintenance workers were absolutely flabbergasted when wild red roses erupted from the depths of the mysterious grave. The prickly plants strangled all vegetation within reach and quickly became a big nuisance. Custodians worked feverishly to tame the unkempt bushes but finally mowed them down out of frustration. However, the spiteful thorn bushes flourished once again and mysteriously seemed to thrive even during the dead of winter.

Yamani, the conquering gardener, removed the roots of the insidious bushes and stuffed the holes with gopher poison. Once the grave was cleared, the Bulgarian maintenance man noticed an unusual tombstone engraved in his home language. Yamani said one of the men buried there was a twenty-seven-year-old man from Austria and that the other was a forty-three-year-old miner from Transylvania (now Romania) by the name of Fodor Glava. The mystery deepened when the maintenance worker noticed that one of the strange words scrawled on the slab spelled "trandofir," which just so happens to be the Romanian word for "rose." Word spread like wildfire, and local "vampireologists" began speculating that perhaps the tree sprouted from a stake that was pounded into Fodor Glava's heart and that the stubborn

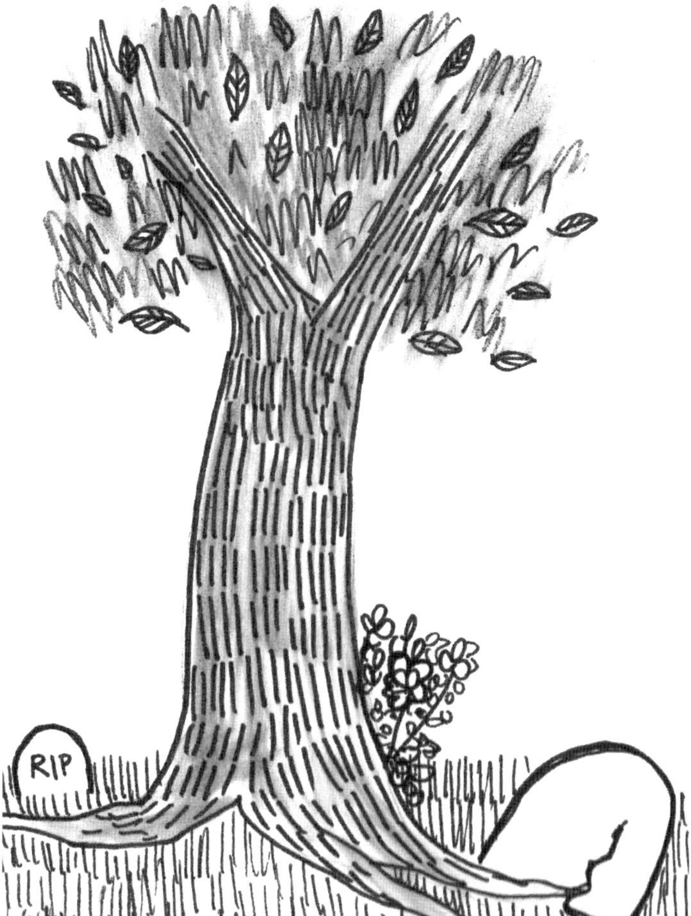
RIP

rose bushes grew from his blood-red fingernails. Ghost hunters confirm that the vampire's grave is haunted and still claim to see the cloaked phantom of Fodor lurking about in the Lafayette cemetery.

Legends of both good and bad witches were popular in Colorado, and believe it or not, one woman was even persecuted for the crime, as headlines in the September 10, 1899 issue of the *Omaha World Herald* shouted, "COLORADO COURT CONVICTS WOMAN OF BEING A WITCH." According to the article, a man had admitted to beating a woman whom he accused of being a witch. The woman went to court, and over a half dozen men stepped forward as witnesses for the prosecution. Raven-haired seductress Catherine Rothenberg was described as being a "beautiful Jewess" who "swayed men with her alluring Arabian charms and mystical oriental spells." Rothenberg had established herself as a well-regarded soothsayer in Leadville, and folks came from all around the country to benefit from the wicked widow's magical powers. One of these people was Martin Roberts, who paid Catherine a king's ransom but demanded his money back when her prediction was wrong. Needless to say, sorceresses don't give refunds, and all hell broke loose when the wicked witch refused. The next day, Mrs. Roberts went to the sorceress's cabin and politely requested reimbursement, but the beautiful witch just mumbled a wicked incantation and slammed the door in her face. Within hours, everyone in the Roberts household fell deathly ill, blaming their misfortune on the witch. For several weeks, the family suffered from all kinds of maladies, but Mr. Roberts refused to beg mercy from the witchy woman. One day, Roberts recalled hearing the vamp tell him that her powers would be vanquished if blood ever spilled from her mouth. That night, Mr. Roberts crept into Catherine's cottage and smacked her on the face until blood was drawn. Alas, she admitted defeat but still refused to refund his money. During the spectacular trial, Sam Jones, the former attorney general of Colorado, became quite incensed when the judge allowed testimony to prove that Catherine Rothenberg was a witch, shouting, "Great God! Is this case being tried in Colorado during the nineteenth century—or are we baiting witches in the seventeenth? I object to the court turning back the hands of time 200 years!" Apparently, his grandstanding worked, and the case was dismissed. Legend holds that Catherine Rothenberg eventually left the mining camp for Denver, where practicing magic was better tolerated.

Sugar Babe was an infamous witch who lived in an old Denver neighborhood called the Bottoms. The haggard, eighty-five-year-old voodoo queen was known to squat in an abandoned boardinghouse located on the corner of Nineteenth and New Haven. The decrepit mansion once had rental rooms upstairs, as well as an early saloon on the main level that was reputed to be haunted by numerous spirits. The ghosts were rumored to be those of three outlaws who died in a gunfight and two sisters rumored to be buried in the basement. The mansion's spooky reputation got plenty of unwanted attention when on June 17, 1920, headlines in the *Denver Post* screamed, "BODY OF MAN IS FOUND DANGLING FROM TWEENTIETH STREET VIADUCT IN FRONT OF HAUNTED BUILDING."

The police assumed that the victim had committed suicide but couldn't be sure since the man didn't leave a note. Old Sugar Babe and her toothless cronies agreed that it was some kind of evil omen. The witches told reporters that the ghosts of the house were angry and demanded three human sacrifices to appease the spirits. Rumors were that the old boardinghouse was being demolished in the name of progress, and a vindictive Sugar Babe was quoted as saying:

> *There got to be three lives pay the price before the ghosts will be content. That body they found Thursday is only the first one. There got to be two more now—murder or suicide or the ghosts won't rest. They've been mighty stirred up about the ruckus about their house.*

Patrolman William Baker was well aware that Sugar Babe's old mansion was haunted, and he used its spooky reputation to his great advantage. The policeman's ingenious idea quickly curtailed crime in the neighborhood and was written about in the *Denver Post* on June 13, 1920, with the following headlines:

HAUNTED HOUSE IS QUICK CURE FOR JAGS, PATROLMAN PROVES

THOSE WHO HAIL FROM "THE BOTTOMS" BECOMING WARY OF IMBIBING TOO FREELY SINCE OFFICER BAKER DISCOVERED STUNT THAT'S BETTER THAN JAIL

According to police records, people living in the Bottoms neighborhood had a penchant for strong drink, yet three weeks had gone by without a single drunk appearing in court—and it wasn't because of Prohibition. The judge was surprised as hell to learn that the policeman had started punishing drunks by making them spend the night in the witch's haunted mansion. The officer was quoted as saying:

> *Everybody down there believes that the house is really haunted. I have warned the old regulars who were in a habit of acquiring a "jag" about once a week that if I found them drunk, I would lock them up in there, and believe me, most of them have stayed sober ever since. Several of them have gotten drunk, and I locked them up there. Five minutes later, they came out absolutely sober.*

Sugar Babe didn't mind a drunken bum squatting at the homestead now and then, but she was furious as hell when the city finally tore down the decrepit eyesore. The demolition squad was admittedly frightened by the intimidating witch, and when a stray mutt dug up a large bone in the basement, it really frazzled them. It was later determined that the dog's buried treasure was just a leg bone from a sheep. Still, other mysterious bones were discovered sticking out of the stone foundation, leading to whispers of satanic worship. The lawmen quickly stifled rumors of human sacrifice by explaining that back in the old days, ground cattle bones were often added to thicken mortar. Needless to say, the workmen were relieved to know that they weren't toiling away in a devil's den. Whatever happened to Sugar Babe after her beloved haunted mansion was razed, nobody really knows, but some folks claimed that the old witch ended up in mystical Manitou Springs.

The mysterious vampire's grave is located in the northwestern section of Pauper's Field in the Lafayette Municipal Cemetery off US 287. For more information, please see www.fullmoonexplorations.com.

For more information on haunted Manitou Springs, please visit www.manitoulegends.com.

Chapter 22

The Living Dead

I'm not afraid of death; I just don't want to be there when it happens.
—Woody Allen

Many of Colorado's mining hubs grew in some unsavory directions during their formative years, and things got even worse after the railroad came through. The mining camps were crawling with all sorts of shady characters, most of whom carried dangerous weapons. Saloons, gambling houses and dance halls far outnumbered churches, and there were definitely more bad guys than good. Once these ruffians got to drinking, all hell would break loose. Needless to say, coffins were in big demand, and undertakers were almost as busy as saloonkeepers. One gruesome story was particularly sad because it occurred just before Christmas. The *Denver Post* recapped the incident in May 1902 with the gruesome headline:

SURREPTITOUSLY SAWED OFF DEAD MAN'S SKULL

The Secret Story of the Acquittal of William Brooks for Killing James Roberts in Cripple Creek Last Christmas

Everyone at the Dawson Club considered James Roberts to be thick headed, but they soon learned otherwise. When the drunkard refused to leave the saloon, the bartender reprimanded him with a thump on the head, and the miner fell to the floor. Figuring that the drunk was playing possum, the revelers went along with the charade, pouring more beer down his throat and propping him in front of the player piano while they danced and sang Christmas carols. After an hour, they finally noticed the blood coming out of the maestro's ear and realized the party was over. The popular bartender was promptly arrested for murder, but all his friends rallied behind him. One friend of the bartender was also the town's doctor, who sawed off James Roberts's head, examined it and testified that the drunkard had an "unusually thin skull," concluding that it was his own darn fault for dying from the thump. The testimony of the undertaker, coroner and many witnesses helped exonerate the beloved bartender, and life went on as usual for everyone—everyone but James Roberts, who was buried without the benefit of ceremony…or a head.

One of the most successful morticians in Teller County was Coroner Dunn, the esteemed president of the Western Association of Undertakers. Mr. Dunn owned the largest and finest undertaking parlor on Victor's Undertaker's Row and made quite a good living off the dead. Mr. Dunn lived upstairs with his wife and children, while the lower level of the massive brick building was used for his business. Although he was not much of a family man, Mr. Dunn was certainly well respected in his field. The undertaker was well known for his understanding of forensics long before it became a reputable science. After a long, rewarding career, the Dunn building sat vacant for many years because people feared its haunted reputation. Finally, the old undertaker's parlor was converted into an apartment building. Despite the fresh paint and shiny new fixtures, most tenants didn't stay long, complaining of a tall shadowy figure that haunted the building with heavy footsteps. Sometimes tenants would awake to feel an invisible force press down on their chest, unable to move or cry for help, and finger-shaped bruises around their necks served as proof of their claims. For a long time, folks were convinced that the malicious energy was the ghost of the undertaker, who even in death wanted to be working in his old digs. Mr. Dunn's former assistant, Mr. Jones, finally broke his conspiracy of silence and spilled the beans about the true identity of the ghost. However, if the dearly departed Mr. Dunn ever found out about the breach of trust, he would surely roll over in his grave!

Jones testified that one time he was assisting Mr. Dunn in preparing the corpse of a mangled miner when the cadaver suddenly twitched on the embalming table. At first, the two men thought their eyes were playing tricks on them and went on with business. A few moments later, the stiff surprisingly came back to life, excitingly flailing his arms and gasping for breath! Mr. Dunn stepped back to collect his wits, and the corpse let out a bloodcurdling howl before bolting upright on the slab. Incredibly, the befuddled dead guy swung off the table and tried to escape before running into the wall and falling flat on his face. No doubt the mangled miner lost his way because his eyeballs were floating in a nearby jar. In all of their years of professional experience, the two men had never encountered a living dead man. Thinking quickly, the maddened mortician hastily plunged a needle into the zombie's arm, causing him to pass out. Mr. Jones said he wanted to get the sheriff but that the creepy undertaker stopped him dead in his tracks and sneered that they didn't need any help from the law. Mr. Jones watched in horror as the maddened doctor hastily stabbed a second dose of morphine into the miner's arm, but he was somewhat relieved when the monster heaved his last breath. Shortly after the mercy killing, all sorts of supernatural activity started happening in the building, but Mr. Jones kept his macabre secret for many years because he was too afraid to come forward with the horrifying truth.

Believe it or not, the strange experience was not the first time that a corpse resurrected itself in a Colorado mountain town. When an avalanche occurred on Homestake Mountain in 1883, a victim was taken to the composing room of the *Leadville Chronicle*. Relatives were called to claim her corpse, but before they arrived, the dead woman got up, brushed herself off and walked right out the door without saying a word to anyone. Just a few of decades later, yet another proclaimed dead guy came back to life in Gunnison. The amazing story was reported in the April 13, 1911 issue of the *Rocky Mountain News* with the following eerie headlines:

THE FESTIVE FUNERAL
A STORY OF HOW THE CORPSE CAME BACK

Everyone in the county was terribly upset upon hearing that popular Sheriff Bowman had been killed by horse thieves in a nearby town, but his young widow was especially besotted with grief. Denver's Bishop Spalding, who just happened to be in town dedicating a new chapel, agreed to stay a few days longer to perform the sheriff's burial service. The widow began planning an elaborate funeral, and the finest casket was ordered from a Denver funeral home. Mrs. Bowman put on her widow weeds, and her home was prepared to receive an onslaught of grieving guests. Friends, neighbors and fellow lawmen all gathered at the sheriff's homestead, and those who could not squeeze inside waited outside, where it was raining cats and dogs. There was not a dry eye in the house—even big, burly mountain men were seen blubbering like overgrown babies. Mrs. Bowman became worried when the hearse was late and was about to cancel the engagement when the rain suddenly stopped—as if on cue. When the guests spotted the black funeral wagon coming, they walked to the road to greet the mournful entourage. When the hearse pulled up, Mrs. Bowman screamed and then promptly fainted in the bishop's arms. In the back of the wagon was the sheriff, sitting on top of his casket! Sheriff Bowman, grinning like a Cheshire cat, stood on top of his casket and deadpanned, "Shame to ruin such a swell funeral, but I refuse to be buried!" At first, a few people were enraged at the sheriff's preposterous joke, but all were soon relieved to see that beloved Sheriff Bowman was still alive and kicking after all.

To see the skull of murder victim James Roberts, please visit the Cripple Creek District Museum. Some folks swear that the miner's skull is haunted, but don't let that silly rumor rattle your bones. You can contact the museum at 719-689-2634.

Chapter 23

Cemeteries and Body Snatchers

Remember friends, as you walk by,
As you are now, so once was I.
Just like me you will someday be,
So prepare yourself to follow into eternity.
—Cemetery epitaph

No one can argue that cemeteries are spooky places, but few people may be aware that Colorado has some of the most haunted cemeteries in the entire country. In Canon City, the wooden markers of the so-called Pecker Hill graveyard were destroyed by woodpeckers long ago. The ravaged headstones were eventually replaced by metal markers made by prison inmates but have long since rusted. Buried here are the long-forgotten executed prisoners from the neighboring Colorado State Penitentiary. Psychics believe that quite a few lost souls still linger on Pecker Hill, tethered there by strong emotions of despair. Many of the prisoners were executed in tortuous ways that are now illegal. Especially feared was the lethal water-torture tank in which the floor would suddenly plunge and catapult the prisoner into the air and often decapitate him. Death row inmate Edward Ives was executed not once but twice. The convicted murderer shouted for joy when the rope snapped off the pulley, setting him free. Eddie thought he could pack his duds and skip home, but it wasn't meant to be. After a second last supper of beans and cornbread, Eddie was strung up once again, but this time the executioner used industrial-strength rope. State records reveal how Eddie Ives struggled for twenty-three minutes before he was finally pronounced dead. The prisoners felt so sorry for Eddie's dumb luck that they all chipped in and bought him the only stone marker on Pecker Hill.

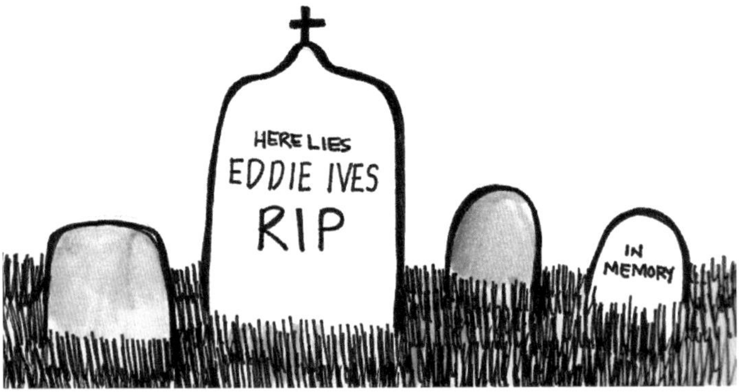

Denver's Chessman Park is also well known for its paranormal activity. Historians will tell you that the beautifully landscaped park was once a city cemetery until urban renewal swept through and claimed the decrepit eyesore. Legend holds that residents were given only a few weeks to find new burial plots, so many graves were plowed over. Years later, it was discovered that an unscrupulous cemetery sexton had robbed graves as they were being relocated. Paranormal investigators suggest that because of this grave disrespect, Chessman is teaming with unsettled spirits. The beautifully manicured lawns and gardens of Chessman Park could be attributed to natural fertilizer. Experts believe that there are at least two thousand bodies still buried under what is now the Denver Botanical Gardens.

The most haunted cemetery in Colorado lies just outside the old mining town of Silver Cliff. For years, old-timers claimed to have seen strange bluish lights in the ancient graveyard, but the mystery finally gained national attention on April 18, 1956, when the haunting headlines of New Jersey's *Trenton Evening Times* screamed, "WEIRD BLUISH GHOST LIGHTS SEEN IN COLORADO CEMETERY."

One night, over fifty witnesses went to the cemetery to observe the spectacular phenomena, and not one of them was disappointed in the spectacular show. Some of the folks tried to catch the mysterious floating balls of energy but were fooled when the light would evade them only to reappear in another section of the forbidden graveyard—as if playing a game of hide-and-seek. One of the witnesses was quoted as saying, "The noticeable thing is that they hover about the tops of the tombstones, depending on how high the tombstones are. I've seen them on the ground and up to head high." In 1968, *Life* magazine featured a full report on the mysterious lights, but its reporters were also at a loss to explain the bizarre occurrence. Residents of Silver Cliff and its Siamese twin town of Westcliffe still claim to see the mysterious ghost lights, and the mystery remains unsolved to this very day.

The most common reason that many ancient cemeteries were protected by tall wrought-iron fences and guarded under lock and key was the fear of body snatchers. With the birth of modern medicine came a huge demand for human corpses. But doctoring the dead was unlawful, so corpses were often purchased by physicians at back-alley doors of hospitals, prisons, mental institutions and poor farms. Obviously, the demand was much higher than the supply, and as a result, grave robbery became a necessary evil. Professional body snatchers became quite adept at pillaging cemeteries and plundering both fresh and long-forgotten graves. Sometimes these scavengers were hunting for buried treasure, while other times, corpses were sought for use in satanic rituals. Occasionally, thieves just wanted a dead body for sentimental reasons. Such was the case when an intense custody battle erupted over the corpse of famous frontier showman Buffalo Bill Cody. Cody wanted to be buried in his namesake town of Cody, Wyoming, but his worried widow had other plans. Mrs. Cody kept her hubby on ice for six long months until his corpse could be interred in a reinforced steel coffin and then secured under ten tons of concrete. During the private funeral, the Colorado National Guard parked an armored tank nearby because the widow feared defiant relatives would actually kidnap the stiff and rebury it in Wyoming.

Several truckloads of concrete were also poured over the grave of Pearl de Vere in Cripple Creek's Mount Pisgah Cemetery. The infamous madam had the most fashionable funeral the state had ever seen. The funeral entourage marched from Pearl's brothel all the way to the Mount Pisgah Cemetery, led by a twenty-piece Elks band and mounted police escort. The thirty-six-year-old redheaded beauty was buried in an exquisite $8,000 pink chiffon ball gown. Sadly, the beloved beauty had died from an accidental overdose the morning after a big shindig. Pearl would likely have been buried in Pauper's Field if it had not been for the generous donation from an anonymous suitor.

The most infamous body snatchers of all time were a couple of misfits by the names of William Burke and William Hare of Edinburgh, Scotland. In 1828, the dynamic duo began murdering innocent people and selling the corpses to Britain's prestigious medical schools. Just ten months later, the duo murdered a popular young street vendor who was recognized on the dissecting table by a local medical student. Legend holds that after the infamous execution, the angry townsfolk ripped the bodies of Burke and Hare limb from limb and then fashioned their dried flesh into souvenir wallets, headbands and buttons.

Colorado is home to a few infamous body-snatching stories as well, and on one occasion, thieves plundering a cemetery near Denver got much more than they ever bargained for. The grave in question belonged to a wealthy old rancher who had apparently died of heart failure—not just once but twice! It was said that the bachelor was buried wearing a fortune in gold. The next morning, an undertaker found three men lying dead inside the plundered grave. Blood was splattered on the inside of the coffin, and the old rancher's chest had been punctured. Investigators surmised that the robbers' spade had breached the coffin and pierced the old man's heart. Scratch marks on the inside of the coffin lid validated the theory that the rancher was mistakenly buried while in a coma, awoke after burial and then attempted to escape the dirt prison. The grave robbers obviously died of fright after hearing the panicked old man scream in agony, as the look of unimaginable fear was immortalized on their faces. When another nearby grave was robbed, the citizens of Denver were terrorized with fear. On November 2, 1902, headlines in the *Denver Post* lamented:

GANG OF HEARTLESS GHOULS ROBBING DENVER'S GRAVES

MUTILATED BODY FOUND ON THE PRAIRE IS IDENTIFIED AS THAT OF DELLA ABBEY, AGED THIRTEEN MONTHS, BURIED ON SATURDAY

Body snatching occurred all over the state but seemed to be especially prevalent in isolated cemeteries in small villages such as Trinidad, where in 1890, a resident told a reporter that his dog had scampered into his kitchen one afternoon with the decayed foot of a child dangling out of its mouth. Authorities followed the muddy trail that led to the city's southern cemetery and found evidence that the fresh grave of a young boy had been violated. Police officers agreed that the grave was likely robbed by a satanic cult, and shocking headlines in the *Denver Post* terrified the town just before Christmas:

GHOULS IN TRINIDAD
THE SOUTHERN CITY IS GREATLY EXCITED ABOUT GHASTLY FIND BY A POLICEMAN…
IT IS SUPPOSED THAT A GANG OF GRAVE ROBBERS HAVE ESTABLISHED THEMSELVES THERE PERMANENTLY

The private Doyle Cemetery, located just south of Pueblo, is one of the most forgotten graveyards in the state. Only a few members of the distinguished Doyle clan were buried there long ago, but now all that remains of the former Casa Blanca Ranch are a few neglected headstones. In 1987, the *Colorado Springs Gazette* featured a fascinating article about Edgar D. Berry, whose great-grandfather, Joseph Bainbridge Lafayette Doyle, was buried on the ranch. Years earlier, Mr. Berry had received a mysterious postcard from a Pueblo historian informing him that his great-grandfather was likely buried with over $1 million back in 1864. Genealogists claimed that after Joseph Doyle died, his young wife, Maria, buried $1 million in gold inside his coffin, as requested in his will. Apparently, the old farmer did not trust banks and wanted, in death, to guard the fortune until his family needed it. Tragically, Maria died not long after her husband. The couple's two young daughters were sent to a convent, and over time, the secret of Casa Blanca Ranch was forgotten. Mr. Berry surmised that the strange postcard was just a weird prank and left it at that. This would later prove to be a grave mistake. After Mr. Berry retired twenty years later, he began investigating his family history and was shocked to discover that there could be some truth behind the mystery. Sadly, when Mr. Berry finally arrived at the remote cemetery, he discovered that he had already been beaten to the treasure. One can only imagine what Mr. Berry was thinking when he tearfully gazed into the vacant grave, but it must have felt something like losing a winning lottery ticket.

Perhaps the most infamous grave robbery in the state occurred in 1906, when a gang of thugs attempted to defraud the Northwestern Mutual Life Insurance Company for thousands of dollars. The lark began when the bloodied, mangled corpse of a miner named John J. McEachern was found near the town of Victor's Mount Straub. Sheriff Bell thought that something seemed fishy about the mining accident, and he grew even more suspicious when Mrs. McEachern refused to identify her husband's corpse. The conniving lawman later returned with a fictitious love letter addressed to her husband, and the widow went wild with jealousy. Mrs. McEachern suddenly blurted out that she was going to claw her husband's eyes out just as soon as she could get her hands on him. After letting the cat out of the bag, the duped woman was promptly arrested. Mrs. McEachern finally admitted to the conspiracy and unwittingly implicated her husband along with five other miners. During the sensational trial, it was revealed that Mr. McEachern and his partners had blown up a recently buried corpse to make it look like a mining accident. However, what the scheming opportunists didn't take into account was that red paint splattered on a rotting corpse would never fool a genuine lawman like Sheriff Bell. Folks in the gold camp were furious with the thugs and wanted to lynch the despicable grave robbers, but despite protests, a hasty trial was held. McEachern was sentenced to life in prison for the foolish prank. Incredibly, just one year into his sentence, the grave robber escaped from prison and found new digs in sunny Mexico.

The grave and museum of William F. Cody can be found on Lookout Mountain Road, just west of Golden.

Madam Pearl de Vere's former Old Homestead is one of only two remaining brothel museums in the entire country and well worth the visit. While in Cripple Creek, you may also want to visit the historic Mount Pisgah Cemetery to see the cement-encased grave of Pearl de Vere. Pearl's many admirers often leave her small tokens of affection.

Chapter 24

Haunted Mines

The boundaries which divide life and death are at best shadowy and vague. Who shall say where one ends and the other begins?
—Edgar Allan Poe

Colorado's roots began in mining, and the industry soon became the backbone of its economy. Sadly, many prospectors were killed in explosions, suffocated by poisonous gas or drowned in the deep, dark caverns of the underworld. Many of the miners in Colorado came from the Old Country with European superstitions and traditional beliefs about ghosts and hauntings. Several spooky stories were spawned from ancient Cornish legends about Tommyknockers. These troll-like supernatural beings sometimes helped the miners by knocking rapidly on the side of the cavern walls to warn of impending doom. However, Tommyknockers also had a devious reputation and were known to steal lanterns, lunch buckets and golden nuggets when the miners weren't looking.

There are many ghost stories about spooky mines in Colorado, and perhaps the most popular center on the Mary Murphy Mine near Leadville, where an explosion killed over one hundred people. Rumors soon began to circulate that the Mary Murphy bunkhouse was also haunted, as noted in the December 18, 1912 *Colorado Springs Gazette* with the following headline: "SAY BUNKHOUSE HAUNTED."

Four miners lodging at the bunkhouse became sick after eating dinner and suddenly died. A wealthy Londoner also became ill after eating the meal and perished a few days after his associates. At first, it was suspected that the men were deliberately poisoned by union activists, but later it was learned that they all had died from ptomaine poisoning after eating bad spinach. Shortly after the deaths, six miners quit their jobs and moved out of the bunkhouse, claiming that it was inhabited by ghosts. The Harding Smelting Plant in Aspen also suffered from a haunted reputation when a Frenchman was killed in a fit of anger by another miner. Shortly after the murder, the Frenchman's ghost was seen by many people, including the night watchman, who was so frightened that he tried to kill the apparition! On November 27, 1892, the *Aspen Daily Leader* headlined:

A SPECTER IN AN ASPEN SMELTER
GHOSTLY SHADE THAT WANDERS ABOUT

DEFYING LEADEN BALL FROM A REVOLVER

With so many haunted mines in Colorado, one might wonder which one had the most diabolical reputation, and ghost-hunting historians would likely agree that the title goes to the Maime Mine near Leadville. From the mine's earliest days, many miners were mutilated in accidents and died within its deep, dark keep, and sometimes their bodies were never found. Miners who worked at the Maime Mine believed that it was home to the devil himself, and legends told of tunnels that were chiseled into sacred Indian burial grounds. Sometimes shadowy creatures would frighten the miners by calling out their names when no one else was around. In the daylight hours, very little was ever said about the mysterious happenings of the underworld mine. However, during hushed whiskey-soaked conversations, a few brave men got up the gumption to confess their concerns about the spook-riddled tomb. Finally, the wearied miners revolted by walking off the job, with only a stubborn few remaining on the skeleton crew. As the prospectors dug deeper and deeper into the mountain, barely audible whispers turned into frighteningly guttural voices, although no one could decipher what they were actually saying. Even more disturbing were the horned figures that fluttered about and would mysteriously vanish into thin air. The most famous ghost story about the Maime Mine began on April 15, 1894, when at 6:00 p.m., an emergency alarm sounded, and the foreman thought he heard his brother-in-law calling for his help. The foreman was bewildered to find out that his bloodied, one-armed brother-in-law had silently climbed out of the service bucket and walked a few yards toward his home before falling dead. A bundle of dynamite had exploded in his hand, and he bled to death before anyone could help. A funeral was held, and everyone who knew the affable man was upset by the tragedy, but the very next day, it was business as usual.

Exactly one week after the tragic death, the foreman heard the emergency bell ring once again at 6:00 p.m. and lifted the service bucket to find a horribly injured miner. The gruesomely mangled body was missing an arm, and the man's unrecognizable face was covered in blood. The foreman reached out to help, but the miner disappeared as soon as he clasped his hand. The foreman nearly fainted when he realized he'd just shaken hands with the ghost of his brother-in-law! The next night at the exact same time, the spooky incident repeated again—only this time the foreman had witnesses. The entire topside crew watched in disbelief as the one-armed ghost crawled out of the bucket and disappeared into thin air. Apparently, several miners below had also seen a bloodied, one-armed man signaling the shaft bucket just before quitting time—they had seen him every night since the miner had been killed. The witnesses explained that they had been too afraid to say anything to anyone.

The awful paranormal scene played out repeatedly over the following months, and rumors about the haunted mine spread far and wide. In the winter of 1894, the overworked miners looked forward to a few days' rest over the holidays. However, on Christmas Day, the topside crew was forced to work after the Maime inexplicably flooded. The crew was hesitant to bail out the shaft using the haunted bucket, but it was the only device they had at their disposal. Strangely, when they lowered the bucket down for the thirteenth time, the cable caught around the foreman's neck, and the other miners watched in absolute horror as he was beheaded right before their very eyes. The spooked miners later found the foreman's hat but never located his head. The headless foreman was buried next to the grave of his one-armed brother-in-law. The miners began calling the haunted mine the Widow Maker, as the Maime continued to take the lives of miners and spit out their ravaged bodies by way of the haunted service bucket. Some old-timers in Leadville still remember haunted tales about the evil mine, but no one ever brings it up—and who can blame them?

Are you planning a trip to Aspen? If so, the spooky Dark Side Tour is a must!

Chapter 25

Spooky Legends

The communication of the dead is tongued with fire beyond the language of the living.
—T.S. Eliot

There have been many books written about Colorado ghost stories—here are a few of my favorite tales:

Indian Curses: It seems that everywhere you look in Colorado, an area is known to have an Indian curse put on it, especially in Meeker. Nathan Meeker had high hopes of building a prosperous community, but despite his good intentions, he got off on the wrong foot with the Indians when he plowed over their racetrack. The mistake ended up costing Meeker his life, as the Indians drove a stake through his heart. After the tragedy, Meeker's ranch was said to be cursed. On July 22, 1900, the *Denver Post* recapped the mystery with the headline,

"DEADLY HOODOO HOVERS OVER THE MEEKER RANCH."

Haunted Rails: In 1885, a locomotive for the Denver, South Park and Pacific was barreling through South Park and nearly plowed into a colossal haystack. When the engineer inspected the tracks, he noticed that there weren't any. Apparently, the train had hydroplaned across the frozen tundra, jumping the tracks somewhere around Fairplay. Crew members drew straws to see which lucky guy got to explain the calamity to the boss man. It might have just been easier to explain that the train was haunted. The dangerous train route over Marshall Pass was well known as being haunted. One cold night as the train approached Marshall Pass, the engineer noticed a rogue train chasing them. More coal was shoveled into the boiler as the locomotive careened through dark tunnels and shook over several bridges, but still the mystery train doggedly pursued and tried to run them off the track! Suddenly, the menacing train tumbled over a cliff. The engineer couldn't believe his eyes! He looked out the window to survey the damage, but the phantom locomotive had disappeared into thin air. According to the *Denver Post*, the engineer found a message scratched into the ice of the engine window that read, "The train that was following you last night was wrecked, and four men were killed. And if you ever run the route again, you too will be wrecked." The foreboding message and ghostly hallucinations emotionally wrecked the engineer, and he soon retired after the inexplicable incident.

Haunted Trees: Old Monarch was a colossal cottonwood tree that once stood at the center of Union Avenue in Pueblo. The tree was once known as the Hanging Tree, as fourteen men had been lynched from its massive branches, and Old Monarch soon gained a haunted reputation. The tree was eventually cut down in the name of progress, but a cross section was preserved and can be seen at the El Pueblo Museum. Another haunted hanging tree is located in Morrison, but the spookiest cottonwood, known as the Hell Tree, is located in La Porte. Legend holds that long ago, a goat farmer murdered his entire family along with all his workers by stringing them up in the tree before hanging himself as well. For more information on the haunted Fort Collins area, please visit www.HauntedFortCollins.com or call 970-372-1445. You can also read the book *Ghosts of Fort Collins*, also published by The History Press.

Creekside Ghost: The ghost of William Tull is known to haunt the shores of East Boulder Creek. The young man was lynched by a mob near the creek for stealing horses in 1867. However, shortly after the necktie party, it was discovered that Tull was actually innocent. For years afterward, local newspapers reported sightings of the ghost of William Hull, a blood-soaked rope hanging from his neck, on the east shore of Boulder Creek. For more information on haunted Boulder, visit www.SpiritBearParanormal.com.

Musician Ghost: Clifford Griffin was a handsome Englishman who moved to Silver Plume to escape a painful past. Clifford's fiancé was murdered on the eve of their wedding, and her killer was never found. Clifford became a successful prospector and built a cabin high above the village of Silver Plume. Every night at sundown, the townsfolk enjoyed hearing the Englishman's lonesome violin recitals echo through the canyon. One summer night just after sundown, Clifford played a beautiful love song, which was followed by the sound of a gunshot. The Englishman was found lying in a shallow grave, dug by his own hand. A nearby marble tombstone had been engraved by the Englishman to include his name, date of birth and date of death—June 19, 1887. The townsfolk held a funeral and buried Griffin as he requested in a suicide note. Shortly after his death, many people saw and heard the violinist near his cabin. Even today, folks swear that the handsome Englishman haunts his grave above Silver Plume, especially around the anniversary of his death.

Fairplay Cemetery Ghosts: Prospector J. Dawson was found dead at the bottom of a mine the summer of 1865. Shortly after the funeral, Dawson's bones were found in the bed of a dancehall girl in Alma. The bones were reburied but reappeared again in the bed of another beautiful young woman. This strange event happened several times over many years, and in 1872, Dawson's bones actually followed a lovely lady into another state! The bones were shipped back to Fairplay, and someone finally threw them into the deep hole of an outhouse. Dawson still haunts the cemetery in Fairplay but has thankfully stayed out of women's beds for the last century. The ghost of Silver Heels is also known to haunt the cemetery near the grave of her fiancé, who died from smallpox. Silver Heels was a dancehall girl who nursed many of the miners with smallpox. After the epidemic passed, the miners took up a collection for the pretty young woman, but she was nowhere to be found. Because of her selfless devotion, the miners named the loveliest mountain near Fairplay Silver Heels, in her honor.

Spooky State Capitol: In 1979, when two mysterious skulls were found in an old crate in the basement of the state capitol, haunted rumors about the building began to make sense. The noggins had apparently belonged to the Espinosa brothers, who ruthlessly murdered nearly thirty white men in retaliation for the Mexican-American War. The brothers were eventually caught and decapitated by Tom Tobin, a scout working out of Fort Garland. Tobin never received a reward for the heads of the outlaws. Perhaps the deprived scout is the restless spirit who still haunts the capitol building. For more information on Denver's haunts, please see *The Haunted Heart of Denver*, also published by The History Press.

Haunted Ludlow: The mining camp of Ludlow was the scene of a violent labor dispute between miners and management. Nearly two dozen innocent people were shot or burned to death, many of them women and children. The Light in the Dark Paranormal team performed an investigation of the Ludlow Massacre site, and their astonishing evidence can be seen at www.lightinthedarkparanormal.wordpress.com/2012/11/01/our-presentation-in-pueblo.

Telegraph Ghost: In the late 1800s, the Palmer Lake telegraph station began receiving phantom messages from Denver, and the mystery was never solved. For more information on the historic Tri Lakes region, please visit www.PalmerDivideHistory.org.

Eddie Needed Coffee: The surprised ground crew struck gold while digging the foundation for the Victor Hotel, and this led to the development of the Gold Coin Mine. The beautiful historic hotel is believed to be haunted by the ghost of Eddie, a miner who lived in the hotel in the 1930s. One morning on his way to work, Eddie somehow fell down the old birdcage elevator shaft to his death. If you are not too afraid, request to stay in Eddie's room.

Littleton Ghosts: On February 25, 1918, headlines of the *Carbonate Chronicle* read, "CRIMINALS SHUN HAUNTED HOOSEGOW." According to the article, prisoners began pleading guilty in order to be sent to the state penitentiary because they were too afraid to spend the night in the city's haunted jail!

Twisted Sisters: Devout spiritualist Alice Crawford haunts Red Stone Castle, where she once lived, and her sister Emma haunts the nearby Red Mountain, where she was once buried. Emma's ghost was so popular with tourists that train tracks were constructed so that visitors could ride to the top of the mountain to visit her grave. Perhaps Emma didn't like getting all the attention and wanted to escape her grave situation. Her coffin washed down the mountain in 1927, and her skeletal remains were found at the bottom of a gulley. Emma was reburied in the Manitou Springs Crystal Hills Cemetery, and many people think that is why she still haunts Red Mountain to this day. On the last Saturday in October, the town of Manitou Springs hosts the Emma Crawford Festival and Coffin Races. For more information please visit www.ManitouLegends.com.

Odds and Ends

Truth is stranger than fiction.
—Lord Byron.

Here are a few strange-but-true forgotten tales that were just too good to leave out:

Headless Chickens: In 1884, the *Denver Post* featured a story about a headless chicken that was exhibited for Denver University medical students. The fowl had been beheaded by Mrs. J.A. Scott of Littleton, but the next day, the headless bird was still struttin' his stuff like nothing ever happened. The students determined that just enough of the chicken's brain stem was left in tact to keep the bird alive. In 1946, the incident happened again when Lloyd Olsen, a farmer in Fruita, decapitated a rowdy rooster named Mike, planning to fry him for Sunday supper. But Mike had other plans and continued to run around the yard like a chicken with his head cut off until the farmer tired of the chase. The next morning, when the farmer saw the cocky rooster trying to peck for food without a head, he naturally felt sorry for the befuddled fowl. Lloyd Olsen kept Mike alive for eighteen months by forcing nutrients down the rooster's throat with an eyedropper. Mike enjoyed his new career and traveled all over the country, meeting new peeps and hanging out with cute chicks. Folks were charged a quarter each to gawk at the headless wonder—and that wasn't just chicken feed back then. "Miracle Mike" was featured in various newspapers and magazines and was even mentioned in the *Guinness Book of World Records*. In 1998, the town of Fruita began hosting the Mike the Chicken Festival, held annually in May.

The Boy With X-Ray Eyes: Doctor Frank W. Brett of Denver stated that when his son Leo was just ten years old, he discovered that he had an amazing talent for seeing straight through things—and he was not speaking figuratively. After going into a trance, Leo Brett could see through clothes, skin, bones, internal organs, muscles, nerves and even the blood pumping through veins. The child's visions were said to be in colorful, graphic detail. On July 3, 1904, the *Denver Post* featured a story with the headline, "BOY WITH X-RAY EYES WHO CAN SEE THROUGH THE BODY. "

Snakes in Sleeping Bags: Native Americans passed down fantastic stories from generation to generation about a strange fire-breathing serpent known as the Culebra de Lumbers, or the fire snake. These legendary serpents killed by spitting fire and searing the vital organs of its victims. Even today, folks will caution campers to zip their bedrolls because the nocturnal monsters like to attack sleepers. Locals will also tell you to never eat yellow snow, but that's a different story.

Shady Ladies: In Cripple Creek, "shady ladies" were given physical examinations once a month, and those who did not comply were fined or thrown in jail. If the soiled dove had children, they were incarcerated along with their mother in the same small cell—for up to one year at a time! For more information on law and order in the Old West, visit the Outlaw and Lawman Jail Museum in Cripple Creek at 136 West Bennett Avenue or call 719-689-6556.

Fish Tales: When a woman lost her wedding ring at Prospect Lake, her husband vowed to find the ring, but she just scoffed at the possibility. When the lake was drained to make repairs in 2004, the woman and her husband went fishing—with a metal detector in hand. The amateur treasure hunters searched only half an hour before finding the wedding ring on the same south shore where it was lost thirty-nine years earlier. There was no doubt that the ring belonged to her, because her engraved name was still legible on the inside rim.

Bad Manners: In 1876, George Harrington was a bartender at Patterson's Saloon in La Junta. One day, a kid walked in and asked for a drink. When George refused, the youngster shot him dead. George has the dubious distinction of being the first man buried in the La Junta Fairview Cemetery.

Tornados: How would you feel if you had just had a fight with your dad over borrowing the wagon only to see him be whisked away to Kansas by a tornado? On June 16, 1917, headlines in the *Pueblo Chieftain* reported, "CLARENCE FANNER'S PARENT PICKED UP BY TORNADO—DIES OF INJURIES."

Radioactive Hot Springs: Colorado is well known for its wealth of natural mineral springs, many of which became hotspots for tourists. With all the hot springs in the state competing for tourist dollars, businessmen had to think of ways to get attention. When traces of radium were found in the water, the industry commercialized it as being very healthy. In Ouray, the hot springs were advertised as being the most radioactive hot springs in the world! On May 1, 1904, headlines in the *Colorado Springs Gazette* rejoiced, "RADIUM IN MANITOU SPRINGS—IMPORTANT DISCOVERY IN MINERAL WATERS."

Dead Guy Hotel Policy: The Sheridan Hotel was built in Telluride in 1891 but burned to the ground just three years later. In 1895, the New Sheridan Hotel was built on the same sight but this time was constructed of brick. Folks were still anxious about staying in the new hotel, so management initiated a new promotion that if you died while spending the night in the hotel, you wouldn't have to pay for your room—or the funeral.

Holy Cow: Since it opened on August 12, 1892, Denver's Brown Palace has never closed. The triangular-shaped hotel was built on a cow pasture owned by its namesake, Henry C. Brown, after Brown had been kicked out of Denver's opulent Windsor Hotel for wearing cowboy boots. The rancher spared no expense building his fine hotel and even had a crematorium built into the building's basement! In 1911, the hotel was the scene of a scandalous high-society murder, and it has been known to be haunted ever since. Every year since 1945, the hotel has hosted a ceremony honoring the stockman's show, during which the prize steer is led into the lobby on a red carpet and persuaded to drink out of the silver championship cup.

Sky High Crapper: Before the days of modern plumbing, the opulent Strater Hotel in Durango featured a unique three-story privy.

The He-Man Women Haters Club: In 1890, Frenchman Luis Dupuy started a successful bakery in Georgetown, which he later turned into a hotel. The establishment became well known as a fine hostelry and restaurant—one where women weren't allowed! On May 18, 1911, headlines for the *Denver Weekly News* marveled, "THE MYSTERY OF LOUIS DUPUY—STORY OF THE HOTEL DE PARIS, WHERE NO WOMAN WAS EVER ALLOWED AS A GUEST." The old hotel is now a museum, and women are now allowed to visit. For more information, please visit www.hoteldeparismuseum.org.

Feather Crowns: When church leader Mary Bryan died in Rocky Ford long ago, everyone knew she was an angel. Their suspicions were confirmed when a feather crown was found inside the old woman's pillow stuffing. Old-timers once believed that when someone died and went to heaven, a crown that looked somewhat like a feathered bird's nest would miraculously appear in the deceased person's pillow.

Alamosa's Prince: On November 25, 1910, headlines in the *Colorado Springs Gazette* read, "CORPSE OF CHINESE PRINCE LOCATED IN ALAMOSA CEMETERY." Apparently, Yllan Chow Cum was a direct descendant of the Ming Dynasty and had to leave the country when he was accused of being insubordinate. Secret Service agents from the United States immigration department searched for the prince for four years before his corpse was discovered in the Alamosa Cemetery. Cum was said to be worth an immense fortune.

Letter from Heaven: On October 8, 1911, jaw-dropping headlines for the *Denver Post* announced, "HOODOO LETTER PURPORTING TO BE FROM CHRIST." The article explained that a chain letter from God had been circulating for thirty years and was even signed by the archangel Gabriel.

The Legend of Mount Shavano: Mount Shavano can be seen near the town of Salida. In the early summer after much of the snow melts, an angel with outstretched wings can be seen on the side of the mountain. Legend holds that the Angel of Mount Shavano was an Indian princess who sacrificed her life by jumping from the summit of the mountain to appease the gods and put an end to a long drought and that the princess's tears formed the lakes, streams and rivers of Colorado. Now every year, the angel appears for a few weeks to remind folks of her sacrifice.

Colorado's First Flag: The laundress jokingly known as "Countess" Katrina Murat is considered to be the Betsy Ross of Colorado, as she was the first to fashion an American flag to fly over the Colorado Territory. Katrina was a daughter of the American Revolution who fashioned the flag from a discarded ball gown and her husband's red long johns.

Bibliography

Asfar, Dan. *Ghost Stories of Colorado*. Auburn, WA: Lone Pine Publishing, 1973.

Bancroft, Caroline. *Silver Queen: The Fabulous Story of Baby Doe*. Boulder, CO: Johnson Publishing Co., 1955.

Barbaro, Barbara J. *Law and Disorder in Colorado City, 1859–1917*. Colorado Springs, CO: Mother's House Publishing, 2009.

The Bishops. *To Create a Castle*. Rye, CO: Bishop Castle, 1982.

Black, Celeste. *The Pearl of Cripple Creek: The Story of Cripple Creek's Famous Madam, Pearl De Vere*. Colorado Springs, CO: Black Bear Publishing, 1997.

Clark, Alexandra Walker. *Colorado's Historic Hotels*. Charleston, SC: The History Press, 2011.

Daters, John, and Lisa Wojna. *Weird, Wacky and Wild Colorado Trivia*. Canada: Blue Bike Books, 2008.

Easterbrook, Jim. *The Time Traveler in Old Colorado*. Colorado Springs, CO: The Great Western Press, 1985.

Eberhart, Perry. *Treasure Tales of the Rockies*. Athens: Ohio University Press, 1969.

Ellis, Amanda. *Legends and Tales of the Rockies*. Colorado Springs, CO: The Denton Printing Co., 1954.

Fay, Abbott. *I Never Knew That About Colorado: A Quaint Volume of Forgotten Lore*. Ouray, CO: Western Reflections Publishing Co., 1997.

———. *More That I Never Knew About Colorado*. Ouray, CO: Western Reflections Publishing Co., 2000.

Franscell, Ron. *The Crime Buff's Guide to the Outlaw Rockies*. Guilford, CT: Morris Publishing Co., 2011.

Friggens, Myriam. *Tales, Trails and Tommyknockers: Stories From Colorado's Past*. Boulder, CO: Johnson Books, 1979.

Gallagher, Jolie Anderson. *A Wild West History of Frontier Colorado: Pioneers, Gunslingers and Cattle Kings on the Eastern Plains*. Charleston, SC: The History Press, 2011.

Getz, Charmaine Ortega. *Weird Colorado: Your Local Guide to Colorado's Local Legends and Best-Kept Secrets*. New York: The Sterling Publishing Company, 2010.

Grout, Pam. *Colorado Curiosities: Quirky Characters, Roadside Oddities and Other Offbeat Stuff*. Guilford, CT: Morris Publishing Co., 2006.

Jessen, Kenneth. *Colorado's Strangest: A Legacy of Bizarre Events and Eccentric People*. Loveland, CO: J.V. Publications, 2005.

Juszak, Lori. *Ghosts of Fort Collins*. Charleston, SC: The History Press, 2012.

Hafnor, John. *Strange But True Colorado: Weird Tales of the Wild West*. Fort Collins, CO: Lone Pine Publishing, 2005.

Hughs, David R. *Historic Old Colorado City*. Colorado Springs, CO: Old Colorado City Historical Society, 1978.

Mackell, Jan. *Brothels, Bordellos and Bad Girls: Prostitution in Colorado, 1860–1930*. Albuquerque: University of New Mexico Press, 2007.

Murphy, Jan. *Mysteries and Legends of Colorado: True Stories of the Unsolved and Unexplained.* Guilford, CT: Globe Pequot Press, 2007.

O'Brien, Christopher. *Enter the Valley*. New York: St. Martin's Press, 1999.

Oldach, Denise. *Here Lies Colorado Springs*. Colorado Springs, CO: Fittjie Brothers Printing, 1995.

Phillips, Bob. *Phillips' Book of Great Thoughts and Funny Sayings.* Wheaton, IL: Tindale House Publishers Inc., 1993.

Schlosser, S.E. *Spooky Colorado: Tales of Hauntings, Strange Happenings and Other Lore.* Gilford, CT: Globe Pequot Press, 2011.

Swanson, Claude, PhD. *The Synchronized Universe: New Science of the Paranormal.* Tucson, AZ: Poseidia Press, 2003.

Turner, Carol. *Notorious San Juans: Wicked Tales from Ouray, San Juan and La Plata Counties.* Charleston, SC: The History Press. 2011.

Waters, Stephanie. *Ghosts of Colorado Springs and Pikes Peak.* Charleston, SC: The History Press, 2012.

———. *Haunted Manitou Springs.* Charleston, SC: The History Press, 2011.

Womack, Linda. *From the Grave: A Roadside Guide to Colorado's Pioneer Cemeteries.* Caldwell, ID: Caxton Press, 1958.

About the Author

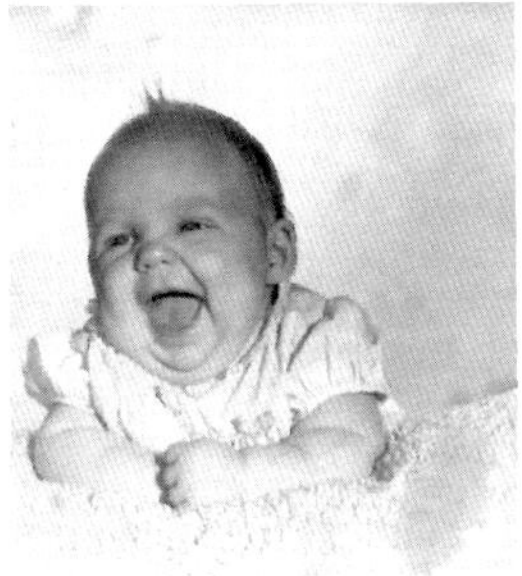

Stephanie Waters grew up in Colorado and has been stretching the blanket since she was just a babe. The armchair philosopher has a degree in liberal arts and a long pedigree of yarn spinners in her family. Stephanie was a professional storyteller before opening a haunted bed-and-breakfast in Manitou Springs. She is also a proud card-carrying member of the Old Colorado City Historical Society and the Adventure Club. The self-described history geek has owned Blue Moon Haunted History Tours and Colorado Ghost Tours LLC since 2002 and sponsors the annual Colorado Paranormal Convention.

Stephanie is the author of *Haunted Manitou Springs* and *Ghosts of Colorado Springs and Pikes Peak*, both published by The History Press. The accidental author was excited to write this book, especially because of her lifelong fascination with the Old West and her relationship to the James gang. Stephanie happens to be a distant relative of James gang member "Windy Jim" Cummins and remembers her great-grandmother, a full-blooded Cherokee, telling her about knowing the outlaw Jesse James. No doubt Stephanie's nefarious heritage is to blame for her unbridled mischief, especially whenever she gets caught dumpster diving or devouring raw meat. Stephanie is also an artist who enjoys finger painting, drinking milk and lukewarm baths.